Christmas Weddings

De-ann Black

Paperback edition published 2023

Christmas Weddings

ISBN: 9798868016226

Christmas Weddings is the fifth book in the Quilting Bee & Tea Shop series.

Also by De-ann Black (Romance, Action/Thrillers & Children's books). See her Amazon Author page or website for further details about her books, screenplays, illustrations and artwork. www.De-annBlack.com

Action/Thrillers:
Knight in Miami.
Agency Agenda.
Love Him Forever.
Someone Worse.
Electric Shadows.
The Strife of Riley.
Shadows of Murder.

Romance:
Christmas Weddings
Fairytale Christmas on the Island
The Cure for Love at Christmas
Vintage Dress Shop on the Island
Scottish Island Fairytale Castle
Scottish Loch Summer Romance
Scottish Island Knitting Bee
Sewing & Mending Cottage
Knitting Shop by the Sea
Colouring Book Cottage
Knitting Cottage
Oops! I'm the Paparazzi, Again
The Bitch-Proof Wedding
Embroidery Cottage
The Dressmaker's Cottage
The Sewing Shop
Heather Park
The Tea Shop by the Sea
The Bookshop by the Seaside
The Sewing Bee
The Quilting Bee

Snow Bells Wedding
Snow Bells Christmas
Summer Sewing Bee
The Chocolatier's Cottage
Christmas Cake Chateau
The Beemaster's Cottage
The Sewing Bee By The Sea
The Flower Hunter's Cottage
The Christmas Knitting Bee
The Sewing Bee & Afternoon Tea
Shed In The City
The Bakery By The Seaside
The Christmas Chocolatier
The Christmas Tea Shop & Bakery
The Bitch-Proof Suit

Colouring books:
Summer Nature. Flower Nature. Summer Garden. Spring Garden. Autumn Garden. Sea Dream. Festive Christmas. Christmas Garden. Flower Bee. Wild Garden. Flower Hunter. Stargazer Space. Christmas Theme. Faerie Garden Spring. Scottish Garden Seasons. Bee Garden.

Embroidery books:
Floral Garden Embroidery Patterns
Floral Spring Embroidery Patterns
Christmas & Winter Embroidery Patterns
Floral Nature Embroidery Designs
Scottish Garden Embroidery Designs

Contents

CHAPTER ONE

'It's snowing!' Kity called to Gordon, looking up at the flakes falling down all around her. She breathed in the fresh sea air, feeling the sense of Christmastime approaching in the beautiful village by the sea on the West Coast of the Scottish Highlands.

Snowflakes settled on the Fair Isle jumper she'd knitted herself using Shetland wool, and sprinkled on her shoulder–length, light copper hair. Her clear green eyes blinked as she gazed up at the icy flakes fluttering down.

Gordon, a fine looking man in his early thirties, was getting ready to put the sandwich board outside his traditional tea shop. He'd written the day's specials that included Scotch broth, Scottish cheddar cheese flan and scones with strawberry jam and cream.

Kity's knitting shop was nearby. Unexpectedly distracted by the snow, she was heading to Minnie's grocery shop further along the esplanade to buy fresh milk and bread.

Some of the shops were converted cottages while others were two–storey premises, creating a niche of little shops on the esplanade. Tucked into the bay that edged the coast, they had a lovely view of the sea.

The main shops included Minnie's grocery shop, Judy and Jock's bar restaurant, Eila's dressmaking shop, Kity's knitting shop, the post office, and Gordon's tea shop where the local quilting bee nights were held. Gordon lived above the shop.

The tea shop was in the heart of the community, and the bee nights were popular with various crafters from quilters to those loving dressmaking, knitting, crochet and embroidery. The bee was the hub of gossip too.

Kity was a recent addition to the community, opening her knitting shop in the autumn and falling in love with Lochlan.

Romance had certainly been in the air the past year and several local couples had found love and happiness in the Scottish village by the sea.

'Maybe I should add jam roly–poly and hot custard to the menu,' said Gordon, thinking that the snowy day merited a warm pudding. 'It started snowing early in November last year too.'

His blue–green eyes viewed the sea. In the milder months, they matched the colour of it, but now the sea looked silvery grey in the winter light. Winter had arrived with frosty mornings and pale sunlight in beautiful grey skies that merged with the sea along the coast. The bay shimmered in shades of silver that highlighted the muted tones of the hills and fields that rose up from the shore.

'No, don't tempt me with tasty puddings,' Kity joked with him. 'I've too much work to do today. A load of new yarn needs unpacking and I haven't even started on the online orders for the Christmas yarn and knitting patterns.'

'How are things going with your new shop? I know you've been open a wee while now, but you seem extra busy these days.'

'Great. Sales have really picked up and there are days when I'm snowed under with online orders for the yarn.'

Gordon looked at the snow falling around her and laughed.

Kity smiled at him. 'The demand for the locally spun and dyed winter range of yarns, especially the Christmas selection has soared. Customers are eager to knit winter woollies. And they're buying my kits to knit a Christmas robin or a snowman.' The kits consisted of Kity's pattern design, with instructions, and enough yarn to make the item. She'd started the kits to help promote her business and now they were helping her profits soar. She packed her orders at the end of every working day and took them along to the little post office. Local customers popped into the knitting shop and bought yarn too, but the online sales kept her very busy.

'I saw that you had lots of lovely pink yarn in your window,' he said.

'Are you thinking of learning to knit?'

'Nooo, I'm happy to hold the bee nights in my tea shop, but knitting and sewing are not for me. I prefer to leave that to you and the other ladies of the bee. I enjoy my baking.'

'And swimming in the sea even when it's raining — or snowing. I saw you take your daily dook early this morning. I shivered just looking at you.'

'It was extra brisk. I didn't know it was going to snow. I might give it a miss on days like this. But I have to say, the sea feels great when it's raining.'

'I'll take your word for it, Gordon.'

Kity's boyfriend, Lochlan, a builder, was a keen swimmer, and although he'd managed to entice her to join him when the water was still relatively warm, she'd drawn the line when the late autumn air brought a hint of winter with it.

Autumn had held its ground well against the onslaught of the winter, and some of the trees higher up on the hillside had refused to part with the last of their copper foliage even as wintertime approached. But she assumed that the burnished leaves would now have their bronze lustre frosted white.

Lochlan would probably still insist on swimming in the sea on snow days to impress her. He'd been trying to impress her since they were at school. Back then, Kity referred to him as *the most annoying boy in the entire world*. A title that even he agreed, as an adult in his early thirties, he merited. He'd only been in love once, and that love burned long and deep for Kity.

Since she'd moved back to the village to open her knitting shop, and he'd returned from a nearby town to help his Uncle Dougal, they'd met properly for the first time in years — and fallen in love. Or as Lochlan put it...*Kity finally fell in love with the boy who'd always loved her*. She did love him. But swimming in the freezing cold sea? Nope. Not happening. If Lochlan went for an icy dook perhaps she would be impressed.

Gordon lowered his voice. 'The reason I'm asking about the pink yarn is...' He glanced to see that Eila, his fiancée, wasn't around. Her dressmaking shop was nearby. She sold the dresses she made, and fabric and thread. 'I'd like to commission you to knit a jumper for Eila's Christmas. I know it's short notice, but—'

'You don't need to commission me,' she cut–in. 'I always knit the new yarns into jumpers and cardigans to promote them, show how nice they knit up, and sell them online.'

Gordon looked hopeful. 'You've got a pink jumper knitted?'

'Better than that. I have a jumper and cardigan set. I only finished sewing the buttons on to the cardigan last night. They're white with pink roses. The yarn is pastel pink. But the soft tone would really suit Eila's pale complexion, blue eyes and blonde hair. She's the same size as me, so they'll fit. Or you can just have the jumper.'

'No, I want the set. That sounds perfect.'

'I'll bring them along to the bee tonight,' she suggested. 'I want to check the finish on the cardigan.'

The bee nights were held in the function room at the back of the tea shop. Patio doors leading out to the garden were opened in the warmer months. Folding tables and chairs were used for the bee, and Gordon allowed the ladies to leave a couple of sewing machines there to make setting up the bee nights easy. Tea, cakes and scones were served and the evenings were popular, held once or twice a week.

'Ideal, but I don't want Eila to see them.'

'She won't,' Kity promised.

'Bill me for them. I'll settle up with you tonight.'

They agreed on their plan and then Kity admired the new frontage of the tea shop. 'I love the new pink theme.'

The shops alongside the harbour were painted in pastel tones including pale strawberry pink, peppermint and cream. Kity's knitting shop was vanilla. The range of yarns she sold provided plenty of colour in her front window.

'Come in from the cold for a moment,' he beckoned, brushing stray snowflakes off his light brown hair. Gordon wore smart black trousers and a white shirt with the sleeves rolled up. He didn't feel the cold, but he could see that Kity was wrapping her arms around herself for warmth.

Kity scurried inside the tea shop out of the snow.

Gordon gestured to the new placemats and napkins and other little touches he'd added to the decor. 'I found old photos in a cupboard upstairs showing that the original decor had a lot of pastel pink, white and cream. I've adjusted a few things to create accents inside the tea shop, but fortunately, most of the vintage lamps have pink glass shades. The walls and ceiling are white and cream and blend well with the pink. I changed the canopy outside the front of the shop, and other wee bits and pieces.'

'It's gorgeous. I've always loved the mix of traditional and modern that you created with the tea shop. And now the pink is sooo pretty.'

Gordon beamed. 'Thank you, Kity. As you know I'm catering for Poppy and Euan's wedding reception soon, and her bridesmaids' dresses and floral theme is pale pink. I'm supplying the food for the wedding buffet that's being held in a marquee, but it gave me the impetus to upgrade the tea shop in time for

Christmas. And I think it'll look lovely for the spring and summer too.'

He'd taken over the tea shop when the previous owners retired and had kept a lot of the traditional styling, adding a few modern elements. But the photos dated back even further and adding pink had been another upgrade to the premises.

'Pink is perfect and works so well with all the seasons.' Kity noticed he had fairy cakes with pink icing in one of his glass display cabinets. Little spotlights highlighted them, along with the glacé fruit tarts.

Gordon noticed her interest. 'I made them for customers and for tonight's bee. They're a new recipe I'm trying for the wedding buffet, so you and the other bee ladies will have to force yourself to taste them.'

Kity pretended to sigh. 'Oh, okay, if you insist.'

The fire burned cosily in the front of the tea shop. The fireplace had the original tiles in floral and cream, and Kity felt the warmth entice her to linger, but...

'I have to get going, but I'll see you later and bring the jumper and cardigan with me.'

'Thanks again, Kity.' Gordon waved her off.

Kity hurried along to Minnie's grocery shop, bringing a flurry of snowflakes with her as she scurried in.

'Is that the snow on?' Minnie had been busy serving customers and tucking her dog Bracken into his basket with a cosy quilt she'd made for him.

Bracken was black, white and brown with floppy ears. He perked up when Kity acknowledged him.

'Morning, Bracken.' She leaned down and patted his head. 'He's got the right idea,' she said to Minnie.

'It's a day for snuggling in by the fire. If only we didn't have our shops to run. Not that I'm complaining. I'm happy with my business.'

Minnie's shop was another hub of local gossip. Neat and tidy, she was in her fifties, wore her brown hair in a bun, and had recently become engaged to Shawn, a mature and strapping farmer. She was a keen quilter and one of the main members of the bee.

Kity picked up a loaf and a pint of milk and placed them on the counter.

Minnie rang the items through the till. 'I love it when it snows.'

'Do you think we'll have a white Christmas?'

'That's the forecast,' Minnie told her. 'There's nothing quite like seeing the shore covered in snow. The hills and fields are blanketed in white in the winter, but when the snow tips off the edge of the esplanade and merges with the sea, it really is magical.'

'I love Christmastime and I'm looking forward to enjoying it here this year,' Kity told her. She'd moved there from one of the towns further along the coast. She had memories of winter in the village when she was a wee girl, and agreed with Minnie's description that it was magical.

'Are you coming along to the bee this evening?' said Minnie.

'Yes. I'm bringing my knitting and my embroidery.' Knitting was her main craft, but she'd been improving her embroidery and quilting skills

8

since joining the bee. Minnie had taught her quilting techniques and needle turn appliqué. And Poppy's expertise in embroidery had been handy to pick up new methods.

'I'll see you later at the bee,' said Minnie, waving as Kity left the shop.

Kity braved the icy breeze blowing in from the sea as she walked back to her knitting shop. The snow was still falling and swirling around her.

She smiled when she noticed that Gordon had added the jam roly–poly and hot custard to his sandwich board.

'Eyeing up the tasty menu?' Judy said, pinning up the lunch menu in the doorway of the bar restaurant next to the tea shop. Judy was in her fifties, trim, fashionably dressed and had her light blonde hair styled to suit her attractive features. She'd found her perfect niche, running the bar restaurant with her husband, Jock. He was a keen ceilidh dancer, and regular ceilidh nights were held there in the function room.

'I already scolded Gordon, telling him I was too busy to be tempted today.'

'We're all busy getting ready for the festive season, and of course Poppy and Euan's wedding.'

'How is Poppy's wedding dress coming along? Every time I meet her, she's bubbling with enthusiasm over the dress you've designed.'

Judy had been a professional dressmaker in the past, though nowadays she considered it a hobby rather than a vocation. The bar restaurant was her shared business with Jock. They had their own house in the village, but Judy still kept the bedroom and living accommodation above the premises. It was handy to pop up and take a break from serving meals and drinks to customers. She indulged her love of dressmaking there too. Her wardrobes were filled with the dresses she'd made, or had bought as vintage pieces that she liked to upscale. She sold her dresses as a sideline, but mainly she just loved dressmaking, and Jock encouraged her. He'd even bought her spare wardrobes. Whenever any of the local ladies needed a dress, Judy was always happy to gift or loan whatever was in her wardrobes that fitted them.

When Poppy described her dream wedding dress at the first bee night after she'd got engaged to Euan, Judy offered to make it for her. Poppy had jumped at the chance, knowing how skilled Judy was, and feeling that this would make her wedding dress even more special.

Fittings were arranged, fabric selected from samples Judy had sent for, the design was made into a toile and from there...Poppy's wedding dress started to take shape.

Kity had yet to take a peek at it, but Poppy made it clear that any of the bee ladies were welcome to have a look at the work in progress.

With Eila being a dressmaker too and owning her own shop, she'd offered to create the dresses for the bridesmaids. More fabric samples were ordered, and at the bee, which was out of bounds to Euan, the satin was whittled down to sky blue or palest pink. It was a tough choice, because the blue was thought to suit the icy winter, but the oyster pink won through. Kity was glad. The pink was her favourite. The bridesmaids so far were Kity, Eila, Judy, Minnie, and Pearl, a local housekeeper in her fifties and part of the bee.

'Do you want to pop in for a peek?' Judy offered. 'You're the only bridesmaid who hasn't seen it yet.'

'Okay.' Kity's tone sounded enthusiastic and she followed Judy inside, through the bar restaurant that had a function room at the back, and upstairs to the bedroom that was more like a sewing room with wardrobes galore.

The dress was displayed on a mannequin in all its satin white beauty. A fine tulle was draped over it for protection and Judy lifted it off to reveal the design.

Kity gasped and stood there for a moment. It was even more beautiful than she'd expected.

'Oh, it's gorgeous.' Kity stepped forward for a closer look, eager to touch the fabric, but kept her hands off it. The pristine white didn't need any other fingers on it except for the expert seamstress.

Judy lifted up an off–cut of the satin and handed it to Kity. 'It's top quality satin, and this is what I've used for the invisible fabric neckline and sleeves.' She gave Kity a piece of the sheer chiffon–like fabric embellished with sparkles that created an effect as if the neckline and shoulders were sprinkled with starlight and snowflakes.

'I love that idea. It looks magical.'

'Poppy loves it too, and it really suits her.' Judy showed Kity photos of a recent fitting.

Kity peered at the pictures on Judy's phone, admiring the close–ups and the back of the dress.

Poppy had a slender but shapely figure and the design looked wonderful on her.

'The back of a wedding dress is as important as the front,' said Judy. 'When Poppy is standing under the bridal arch in the marquee beside Euan, all eyes will be on the rear view of the wedding dress.'

'You're right. I never considered that.' Kity sounded thoughtful. At the bee nights, she liked picking up tips from the other skilled members, including Judy.

'I'm working on embellishing the bodice with crystals. Poppy drops by most days to work on the embroidery. I'm helping with that too. I like embroidering motifs on to my clothes.'

Kity looked at the intricate white floral embroidery work on the dress that included lily of the valley. 'The embroidery is lovely.' Poppy and Euan's names were subtly part of the design.

The invisible fabric sleeves were full–length with scalloped edges tapering down to the wrists.

'The date of the wedding is still to be embroidered,' Judy explained. 'Poppy is stitching it into the sleeves, entwining it with floral embroidery.'

'That's a lovely touch.'

'Yes, and as Poppy is such an expert at embroidery, it'll be as subtle as the names.'

Kity had been so fascinated with the wedding dress that she hadn't noticed Judy's bridesmaid dress was hanging up on a rail.

Judy gestured to the oyster pink satin dress. 'I've finished my dress.'

Kity went over for a look. 'I thought Eila was making all the dresses for the bridesmaids.'

'She was, but then I thought I could help by making mine. Eila gave me a copy of the pattern and...here it is. Eila's finished making her dress too, and Minnie and Pearl have offered to hem their dresses, so that just leaves your dress to be done.'

'I really want to improve my sewing and dressmaking. Seeing what you've made, it makes me want to start having a go at making my own clothes. I knit all my own jumpers and cardigans. It would be handy to make dresses too.'

'I'm always stitching something, so come round and I'll teach you.'

'I don't want to put you to any bother, Judy.'

'Nonsense. I'd make dresses all day if Jock didn't need me to help with the bar restaurant. I've loved sewing since I was a wee girl. It's such a useful skill and a wonderful hobby. I find it relaxing and exciting.'

'I know what you mean. I get that when I'm knitting. I love trying new yarn, new patterns, and the actual knitting is so relaxing.'

Judy draped the covering over the wedding dress again. 'Poppy is embroidering her veil with florals to match the dress.' She showed Kity her sketch book of designs. Fashion drawings. Wedding dress designs.

Kity was taken aback. 'Did you sketch all of these?'

'Yes. Whenever I get an idea for a dress, I add it to my sketch books. This one has wedding dress designs.' She pointed to a shelf where other sketch books were lined up. 'I've got books for various designs — vintage tea dresses, cocktail numbers, tartan dresses for the ceilidh dancing, fashionable day dresses.'

'Your artwork is amazing. I love fashion drawings.' Kity looked through the sketch book at the wedding dress designs and notes and stopped at one of them. 'This wedding dress is so classy.' It was a traditional style with a soft flowing skirt.

'What type of dress would you like for your wedding?'

Kity held up her empty ring finger. 'I'm not even engaged yet.'

'I know, but don't you have a dream dress in mind? Poppy said she'd always wanted to be a Christmas bride and have a dress with the bodice encrusted with snow crystals and a full satin skirt. The invisible neckline and sleeves were my suggestion. But she says it's what she'd had in mind since she was little.'

Kity sighed. 'In an ideal world, my perfect dress would be white chiffon rather than satin. I love Poppy's dress, but soft and light as air is more my style. And I'd like a veil that wafted too. Dreamlike I suppose. But I'd like a small, intimate wedding. Nothing too fancy. I don't think I could cope with all the planning for a large ceremony and reception. I'd be happy with a beautiful dress, a wedding cake, and the man of my dreams. And it would be great to be a Christmas or winter bride. Winter is my favourite season. That's why I'm so excited to be a bridesmaid at Poppy's wedding. Christmas weddings are gorgeous. I've attended a few, but I've never been a bridesmaid.'

'Maybe you and Lochlan will get married next December,' Judy suggested. 'Though we've all seen the way he looks at you. He might want to propose in the New Year and you'll be a spring bride.'

Kity blushed. 'We haven't even talked about getting married yet.'

Judy smiled. 'Well, we'll see.'

Kity picked up her shopping bag. 'I'd better get going. I've a fair bit of work to get done today. Thanks for letting me see Poppy's dress and your sketches.'

'Remember, Euan is to know nothing about the dress,' Judy said as she led Kity downstairs.

'I won't say anything.'

'What have you two been up to?' Jock smiled cheerily at them as he stood at the well–stocked bar. Behind him the array of bottles ranged from whisky to brandy, and there was a selection of liqueurs for making cocktails. Everything shone in the morning light and reflected in the mirrors that lined the shelves and along the bar area. Spotlights highlighted the bar restaurant that served lunches and dinners to local customers and visitors to the area. At the back of the premises was the function room with a fair size dance floor where the party nights were held.

'I was showing Kity the wedding dress and my bridesmaid dress,' Judy told him.

'I hear that Poppy's dress is beautiful,' said Jock, a sturdy and fit man in his fifties with a liking for wearing a kilt at every opportunity, especially for the ceilidh dancing. 'I'm not allowed to peek at it so I don't blab any details to Euan. Not that I would intentionally, but Judy knows sometimes I blurt things out.'

'It is beautiful,' Kity confirmed. 'And so is Judy's dress.'

'I've seen that, and yes, it's lovely. I think it's going to be a wonderful wedding. I'm planning a few special items for the reception buffet menu along with Gordon.'

'Gordon's serving jam roly–poly and hot custard at the tea shop today,' Judy told him. 'Maybe we should add a warm pudding to our lunch menu.'

'I'll rustle up chocolate pudding with hot chocolate sauce.' Beaming with enthusiasm, Jock bustled away through to the kitchen.

Picking up a pen from the bar, Judy accompanied Kity out. 'I'd better add chocolate pudding to the menu.'

They walked outside.

'Thanks again for showing me the dresses,' Kity said to Judy.

Judy wrote the added temptation to the menu that was pinned up on the door. 'See you tonight at the bee.'

Waving, Kity headed along to her knitting shop.

Hurrying inside, she went upstairs to where she lived above the shop. Her kitchen was small but cosy.

She'd decorated everything in a vintage style and painted the walls in ice cream colours — vanilla for the living room, pale strawberry pink for the bedroom, a peppermint bathroom, and cookie dough cream for the kitchen accentuated with pistachio.

She'd bought second–hand items of furniture including a little kitchen table and chairs. The quilting bee ladies had given her quilts for her bed and the sofa, cushions with flower, fruit and butterfly appliqué, and floral print curtains for the windows to match each room's colour scheme. Their gifts made her feel so welcome.

Minnie had shown her how to make appliqué cushion covers of her own, and now Kity's hand stitched seahorse design was part of the decor.

Sitting at the kitchen table having tea and toast for a late breakfast, she looked out the window at her back garden. There was a light dusting of snow on the grass, the apple tree, sparse greenery and her shed. Beyond her garden she saw Euan's flower fields, including the one he owned that had Embroidery Cottage in part of it.

Euan, a flower grower, owned four fields. Inherited wealth accounted for a substantial part of his money, but he worked hard cultivating his fields and lived in a large, two–storey farmhouse tucked into the far side of the main field. He'd purchased the fourth field when the farm owners retired. It included a cottage with a garden.

Poppy moved into the cottage earlier in the year. As her business was embroidery, it was now called *Embroidery Cottage.*

Euan had advertised the cottage for lease.

Poppy left the city to start a new life in the village and build up her embroidery business selling her patterns and embroidery thread.

She'd fallen in love with Euan and they were due to be married ten days before Christmas. Poppy had always wanted to be a Christmas bride, but the last thing she'd expected when moving to the village was that she'd fall in love with rich and handsome Euan, owner of the flower fields, a lovely farmhouse and the cottage. But now the wedding was set to be held in a marquee in the main flower field, catered for by Gordon with help from Jock.

Everyone close to the couple in the community was chipping in to help with everything from the catering to the dressmaking.

Kity was looking forward to the bee night. Lots of wedding sewing was planned.

Sipping her tea and eating her hot buttered toast, she watched the flower fields start to look like a picturesque Christmas card.

Embroidery Cottage was slowly disappearing into the snow scene. The roof was iced white and now blended with the pretty whitewashed cottage.

CHAPTER TWO

Poppy glanced out the window of Embroidery Cottage and blinked. She'd been so busy working on her new embroidery patterns that she hadn't realised it was snowing. Working from home suited her and most of her sales came from online orders. Sales of her autumn embroidery patterns and thread had recently given way to Christmas and winter patterns.

Floral designs were always her top sellers whatever the season, but there had been an increase in demand for Christmas roses, winter pansies, poinsettia, holly, snowbells and other festive flowers. In addition, her Christmas tree, sleigh and gingerbread house designs were selling well too.

She'd previously worked for a management company in Glasgow, but at thirty–one, she'd left that life behind for a fresh start to live and work in the village. She sold her patterns and her embroidery kits from her website.

Her cute cottage patterns were a recent addition to her designs, and she'd spent the morning embroidering one depicting a snowy cottage in the depths of winter. She'd set up her camera and filmed herself satin stitching the roof with crewel wool, and using stranded cotton thread to embroider the walls, door and windows.

Embroidery Cottage was painted white with pink window frames and a pink door, and she'd used those colours for her design, not knowing that outside it had started snowing.

Perfect, she thought, looking out the window of the living room. A wintry grey sky stretched over her garden, the flower fields and down to the sea. A narrow pathway led to the shore and she could walk to the shops in minutes. Or she could drive down along the road that led all the way from the esplanade up into the hills and forest. From the forest, the road continued on to the main routes to two nearby towns and the city. The towns were on either side of the village but far enough away to create a haven of village beauty. But it was a lively community and she'd made more friends there in a short while than in a lifetime spent in the city. The bee was a large part of the welcoming vibe, and she'd been swept into the warm–hearted crafting nights by Minnie, Judy and others. Now, she wouldn't dream of going back to her previous life. This was where she felt at home.

A log fire burned in the hearth and she'd been sitting in her comfy chair at her sewing table near the window stitching the pattern on to white cotton fabric in a seven inch hoop. She liked to sit near the window to sew in the natural light, but as the winter days were often overcast, she had a lamp to illuminate her work area. She'd only been using it for sewing in the evenings, but as the daylight hours dwindled in winter she tended to have it on all day.

Nearer the fire was an antique writing desk from Euan's farmhouse. This was her artwork area. She'd set up her lightbox for inking her artwork and for tracing patterns on to fabric ready for embroidering. Dookits held her pencils and pens that she used to ink her illustrations.

Her videos demonstrated her embroidery techniques and brought in more sales for her products. Customers downloaded her patterns from her website, and she posted out her kits from the local post office. The kits included cotton and linen fabric cut to the required size, thread and the pattern. On her website were pattern templates, detailed sewing instructions, information on the stitches and threads, pictures of the embroideries being worked and the finished designs.

Recently, she'd updated her website news letting customers know that she was taking a break from mid–December. A Christmas break until the New Year. She explained that she was getting married ten days before Christmas, so all orders would be posted out before that. This had brought in a rush of orders from customers, and she'd packed another pile of kits that morning ready to be taken to the post office later.

Snow swirled past the living room window and she put her work aside, excited to see the front garden scattered with icy flakes.

Hurrying to the front door, she stepped out into the snowy day, wrapping her arms around herself for warmth, determined to breathe in the cold, fresh air and enjoy the first snow of winter.

She wore cords tucked into her slipper boots and a long–sleeve top. Her chestnut hair hung around her shoulders and was soon speckled with snowflakes. The pale grey tones of the landscape matched her eyes, and she blinked against the flakes, seeing Euan emerge from his farmhouse in the distance. He waved as he made his way across the flower fields towards her cottage.

Striding across the fields, he was a strapping figure in his thirties. In the winter months he spent a lot of his time planning for the early spring, tidying the fields and cultivating the hardy winter plants and foliage that were popular at Christmastime.

As he approached she welcomed him with a hug and a kiss then led him inside the cosy cottage.

Euan was so tall he had to slightly dip his head to step inside the doorway, especially when he was wearing his sturdy boots that were ideal for trudging about in his fields. But once inside the hallway, he stood upright and shook the snow from his jacket. Euan had a penchant for wearing expensive casuals in neutral tones, and his moss green cords were teamed with an ochre jumper.

'Anything secret that I'm not supposed to see?' he said.

'No, nothing. My wedding dress is safely out of view in Judy's sewing room, and the bridesmaids' dresses are in Eila's dress shop, so it's a bridal–free zone this morning.'

Euan had a handsome face with strong features, burnished gold hair and hazel eyes that took everything in. He smiled and admired Poppy, taking her in, and pulled her close for a second round of hugs and kisses.

Poppy then led him through to the living room.

'When I saw the snow, I wanted to make sure you had enough logs and kindling for the fire,' he said.

'I think I have plenty, but I'm probably going to be lighting the fire most days now that the winter has notched up into the freezing zone.'

'I'll bring some more to keep you well stocked,' he assured her. Then he glanced at the pile of packages for posting. 'I see you've been busy. I'm heading down to Minnie's shop. Do you want me to hand these into the post office for you?'

'Yes, that would be great. I've been filming a new video and that would let me get it edited and uploaded on to my website. And I've lots of other patterns to finish and fuss with. The Christmas designs have been so popular.' She took a deep breath. 'And things to do for the wedding.' A large folder and a wedding planner journal sat on top of the dresser.

He pulled her close and gazed down into her pale grey eyes. 'I've organised the marquee, and I've held plenty of party events in my field, so you don't have to worry about that.' He had a few lads that worked the fields for him and they always helped to put the marquees up, and other locals were helping too.

'I'm going to the bee tonight, so I'll speak to Gordon about the wedding cake and the buffet. The ladies are helping with the accessories for the bridesmaids, including the knitted boleros, and with the favours — little hand sewn bags to hold the flower seed packets, and lots of pretty floral cotton drawstring bags for the embroidery threads, paper patterns and thimbles.' They'd themed their favours for the guests between Euan's flower growing and Poppy's embroidery. 'They're making quilted coasters, knitted wedding bells and knitted hearts too. Plus we'll have miniature bottles of whisky and Scottish tablet in bags as favours.' She took another deep breath. 'So everything is going according to plan.'

'Then you can relax a little.' His voice sounded soothing.

'I think I'm just excited about...getting married!'

Euan's smile warmed her heart. 'So am I. I couldn't be happier. Pearl's been fussing with the farmhouse.' He hired Pearl as his housekeeper, and although she had a few clients in the local area, she was determined to make the farmhouse perfect for Euan and Poppy. 'Apparently, it needs a few things sorted out to make it more welcoming for you.'

'I think your farmhouse is lovely. It's very you.'

'Well, Pearl is making it slightly less me and more for us as a couple.'

'Awe, I love that.'

'So I'm leaving her to it. I'm sure she'll add little touches to make it nice for after the wedding.' He gazed lovingly at her. 'Are you sure you don't want me to whisk you away on a honeymoon to somewhere hot and sunny?'

'No, I love the winter, and now that it's snowing, it's even more perfect. I really don't want to spend our first Christmas somewhere else. I'd rather be here, at home.'

'I would too, but I just wanted to make sure.'

On her tip toes she gave him a reassuring kiss. 'If this snow continues into December—'

'That's the forecast,' he cut–in.

'We'll be snowed–in together.' She gave him a mischievous smile.

'Oh, how awful,' he joked. 'Whatever will we do to pass the time?'

'Snuggle in front of the fire, bake cakes, eat tasty dinners, cosy up on the sofa and watch Christmas films.'

'It sounds perfect.' He almost lifted her off her feet with the loving hug he gave her. 'Okay, I'm going to head down to the post office and the shops. Keep cosy.'

'I will.' She put the parcels in a bag to protect them from the onslaught of snow, handed the bag to Euan and walked with him to the door.

He paused in the hallway. 'Are we still on for lunch?'

'A late lunch. It's bee night,' she reminded him.

He remembered. 'I know. So I'll drop by in the afternoon.'

'Yes, that would give me a chance to get on with the orders and the designs. Then we can have lunch. I'll pop a savoury pie in the oven.' And before she knew it, the day would've flown in and it would be time to get ready for the bee.

It started at seven and many of the ladies were there at six–thirty to set up the sewing machines and organise the tables and chairs. Having dinner at teatime didn't suit those evenings. Gordon spoiled them with tea, scones, cakes and other delights, so she preferred to eat a light meal in the afternoon so she had an appetite for the tasty treats. And they weren't all sweet. Gordon often included savoury snacks — cheese pastries, potato wedges, mini quiche, buttered baguette, cheese scones and sausage rolls. Many of these popular treats were making their way on to the wedding buffet menu.

'I'll see you later,' said Euan. 'And if you look out the window and notice a snowman tending the flower fields today, give me a wave.'

Poppy laughed and reached up to tug the collar of his jacket around his neck and adjust his scarf to keep the cold out.

Euan leaned down and kissed her then opened the front door.

An icy gust blew in bringing a flurry of flakes with it.

'Close the door. Don't let the heat out.' And off he went, striding away down the garden path, across the flower field towards the shore, carrying the parcels.

Poppy shut the snow out and hurried through to the living room to watch him. Her front garden merged with the field, but Euan had made sure that the garden had plenty of flowers, including those that were evergreen or hardy to stand up against the winter. A tree stood beside the cottage and on the other side was a floral arch.

The wisteria that clambered around the front door and windows had been pruned, but the clematis was hanging tough around the arch. The hedgerows that bordered the garden were mixed with thicket and thistles. And the red robin hedging gave a splash of bright colour.

Winter had pared most things to the bone, but Euan's choices of flowers and shrubbery had kept her garden lovely. It wasn't full of flowers like it had been in autumn, but it wasn't sparse. Holly and berries, winter jasmine and hardy little pansies were holding strong against the cold. Euan had cultivated other flowers too, many that she photographed and used for her patterns, including snowbells, heather, jingle bells clematis, winter's snowman camellia and winter bells hellebore.

As the snow covered the landscape in a light layer of white, she watched Euan's figure become a blur in the distance and then he disappeared from view.

Sitting back down in the cosy living room with its traditional chintz sofa and chairs and comforting fire, she continued with her embroidery work for a short time and then stopped. Inspired by the snow covering her garden in a measurable layer of flakes, she decided to capture a few minutes on film with her phone to show her customers the beauty of Embroidery Cottage in the depths of winter.

Putting a cosy knit cardigan on over her top, and a pair of boots, she ventured outside and gave a swift tour of the garden scenery, highlighting the flowers that were available as patterns, and showing the florals in all their winter beauty.

'The air is so fresh,' she said, walking across the lawn to show the border plants, the tree and the archway. 'The sense of snow is amazing mingling with the icy breeze wafting up from the sea. It's invigorating!'

Excitement charged through her, boosting her energy, probably from the impromptu visit from Euan, thoughts of her impending marriage, and the wonders of her surroundings. She couldn't ever picture moving back to her corporate life in the city.

'Okay, I'm heading inside now to embroider by the fire and have a cup of tea.'

Clicking her phone off, she looked at the view, let the snowflakes kiss her face, took another bolstering breath of the freshest air imaginable, went back inside her cottage and did exactly what she'd said she intended to do.

After dropping Poppy's parcels off at the post office, Euan headed to Minnie's grocery shop. Bracken wagged his tail but made no move to get up from his cosy basket as Euan leaned down and ruffled his fur. In the warmer months, Euan sometimes took Bracken for a jaunt down the shore when Minnie was busy with her shop.

Pearl was there buying her weekly shopping and the chatter was edged with the latest gossip.

'Abby and Josh have flown to Dublin,' Minnie said to Euan, as if he was supposed to know the ins and outs of another of the village's romances.

'Oh, very nice,' Euan remarked. He knew Josh and Abby. Two large mansions were perched on the hillside. Josh owned one of them. He was a lawyer, businessman investor, and was renowned for his boxing training, often running along the shore in all weathers to keep strong and fit. He got on well with Josh, and with Abby. She'd moved from the city, like a few others, including Poppy, to start afresh by the sea. Her reasons revolved around taking over her great aunt's bakery cottage. The deal involved Abby only being able to sell the cottage after living and working there for at least a year. Abby hadn't anticipated falling under the spell of Josh, renowned as a man who kept himself to himself. But now they'd become a couple like Poppy and him, and Gordon and Eila. Euan nodded thoughtfully to himself. It was true what Minnie and others said. There were times when romance was rife in the village. He'd no complaints considering he was part of the lucky couples.

Euan didn't know what was going on with Abby and Josh, but he smiled politely on hearing the latest revelation.

Pearl knew Euan's reaction from having tended his farmhouse for quite a while now.

'We all thought Abby and Josh would be the first of the new couples to get married this year. At Christmas,' Pearl explained to Euan, bringing him up to date on the gossip and speculation.

'Ah, so now they've run off to Dublin there's no hint of a Christmas wedding for them,' he surmised.

'Nooo,' Pearl corrected him. 'They recently said they were getting married in the New Year.'

Euan was lost. 'So what's the issue with them being away in Dublin?'

Minnie explained to him. 'Abby was planning to be one of Poppy's bridesmaids if she was available at Christmas. Eila aimed to run up a dress for her. It seemed like they'd be settled here for Christmas.'

Pearl picked up the story. 'But Abby's just messaged Minnie and said they've arrived in Dublin. Abby thought they were having a quick trip, a few days in Edinburgh for Josh's business deals, but whatever happened, they've jaunted off to Dublin.'

'Abby says that Josh has booked them into a lovely hotel in the city centre, and that she's not sure whether they'll spend Christmas there,' Minnie elaborated.

'Right, well, it sounds very spur of the moment but romantic,' Euan said tactfully.

'It is,' Pearl confirmed. 'So now the bridesmaids are Kity, Eila, Judy, Minnie and me.'

Minnie nodded and continued to put Pearl's shopping through the till.

'Five bridesmaids it is then.' Euan tried to sound satisfied with this. He didn't dare admit that he hadn't realised the wedding plan had wiggle room for six. Then again, Poppy was the one with the folder filled with all the wedding plans. He'd taken care of everything he'd promised to do. The marquee with a dance floor, tables for the buffet, fairy lights galore for the ceremony under the floral arch and sprinkled like stardust inside the marquee. He'd done it all. Everything was set.

He'd offered at every opportunity to help with anything else Poppy wanted. But somehow...Abby the bridesmaid on standby hadn't registered with him.

Something told him it was better to keep that under his hat, so he buttoned his lips. Confessing to Poppy at a later date would make for a quirky story when they looked back on their happy day.

Minnie stopped dealing with the groceries and held up her phone to show Euan the pictures that Abby had sent with her message.

'This is Abby and Josh standing on the Ha'penny Bridge in Dublin. It's over the River Liffey in the heart of the city,' Minnie explained while he looked at the pictures. 'And this is them in the Temple Bar area. It's bustling with activity and the cobbled streets mixed with the modern aspects look lovely.'

'Dublin is great,' said Euan. 'It's a few years since I was there, but I enjoyed it. I'm sure they'll have a great time.'

'Josh has business meetings set up, so although they'll have lots of time together, Abby plans to scoot around the shops,' Pearl added.

'We're thinking they won't be home in time for Christmas,' Minnie told him.

'Well, it'll be like a honeymoon in advance before they get married in the New Year,' said Euan.

Minnie and Pearl blinked. This thought hadn't occurred to them.

'You're right, Euan,' said Minnie.

'I never thought of it like that,' Pearl agreed.

Neither had Euan until the words popped out of his mouth. But it seemed to allay their concerns about Abby and Josh missing Christmas in the village.

'A pre–wedding honeymoon.' Minnie nodded firmly, giving the situation a positive sounding name.

'What a great idea. And as you say, Euan, so romantic,' Pearl added.

Feeling he'd earned himself a few good points, Euan quit while he was ahead. He went to leave.

'Wait!' Minnie called to him.

His heart jolted, wondering if he'd done anything wrong. But no.

'You came in for something,' Minnie reminded him. 'Don't let Pearl's load of shopping hold you up.'

'You're welcome to buy what you need,' said Pearl. 'I'm in no particular hurry.'

'Right, I eh...I came in for milk, cheese, bread and cake.' He rattled off the items he'd mentally listed he needed for that evening at home in the farmhouse and for lunch with Poppy. The cake was to share with her.

'What type of cake?' Minnie pointed to the bakery tray on the counter offering fruit cake, raspberry sponge with fresh cream and a chocolate Yule log.

He eyed the tasty selection. 'I know it's snowing, but isn't it a bit too early for Yule log?'

'Gordon's trying out a new recipe. It has oodles more chocolate buttercream. He insisted I try it out on my customers. You'd be the first to taste it.'

Backed into a corner he was happy to be in, he lifted the Yule log and placed it on the counter.

Meanwhile, Pearl, knowing his tastes, was selecting his Scottish cheddar cheese along with milk from the fridge and a loaf of fresh baked bread.

He was happy to let her take charge. She often restocked his cupboards when he was busy and knew his tastes better than he did.

Pearl added a tub of sea salt and a packet of his favourite shortbread. 'You're out of salt and there's no shortbread left in your biscuit tin.'

Yes, Pearl was spot on, he thought.

'And I've rearranged some of the furniture in your bedroom to make room for Poppy's things, and hung padded coat hangers in the wardrobe for her nice dresses and tops. They're the hangers I make myself from my quilt fabric scraps. And I moved your summer clothes through to the other wardrobe in the spare bedroom. You won't need those until the spring.'

Euan tried to look after himself. He did. But there were times when it wasn't viable timewise to forgo the work in his fields, or business accounts, to tend to his attire and other things. He'd become accustomed to Pearl looking out for him, though when Poppy moved in as his wife, he was determined to pull his full weight to share the tasks as a married couple.

'Put the last of Pearl's shopping through the till,' he said to Minnie, indicating he was in no rush.

Minnie rang the remainder of the items through, from tinned broth and a bag of potatoes to butter and porridge oats.

Pearl went to pay for her shopping, but Euan stepped in front. 'Add everything to my bill,' he said to Minnie.

'Oh, that's very generous of you, Euan.' Pearl was taken aback, but she'd known nothing but kindness from him over the few years she'd done his housekeeping. Poppy had found herself a good–hearted man.

'Thank you for all your help with the farmhouse, Pearl,' he said.

Pearl smiled at him and picked up her shopping bags. 'I'll see you later tonight at the bee,' Pearl said to Minnie and headed out happy with her gifted groceries.

Minnie smiled at Euan. He was wealthy, but was always the first to chip in to help the community. A week's worth of groceries was a handy gesture to Pearl. She lived on her own and although she had adequate work doing housekeeping locally, this was a welcome boost.

'I meant to ask,' he said, 'I'd like a new quilt for my bed. One of those beautiful patchwork quilts you or the other ladies make would be ideal.'

Minnie bagged his shopping and pressed her lips together firmly.

Had he said something wrong?

'And I'd like new cushion covers like the ones you make at the bee. I think you made some for Kity when she first arrived here,' he added.

Minnie kept her expression firm and her lips sealed.

'Have I said something out of turn, Minnie?'

'No, nothing.' She didn't elaborate.

This made him worry more. There was definitely something amiss. But what? Surely they'd be happy to supply quilts and other items for his farmhouse. They were always making them, and sold them from the bee's website.

'Should I buy them direct from the members' website?' he said tentatively.

'No, I wouldn't do that, Euan.' Minnie gave him a knowing look.

He still didn't get it.

She increased the intensity. 'You never know what you'll get as wedding gifts.' She said no more.

The penny dropped and rattled around his brain. 'Oh, I see, so—'

'Nothing, Euan.'

'Okay.' He said no more this time. The women had clearly planned a wedding quilt as they had for other couples he'd heard of. Now it was Poppy and his turn to be on the receiving end of their gifts. He smiled to himself as he picked up his shopping and headed out.

'I know nothing,' he said to Minnie.

She smiled at him and waved him off.

The blustery day blew around Euan the moment he stepped out of Minnie's shop and he heard someone call to him from further along the esplanade.

'Ah, Euan, just the man I wanted to see.' Jock bounded towards him from the bar restaurant.

Euan had no idea what Jock wanted, but walked along to him, buffeted by the sea air and snow.

CHAPTER THREE

'Dancing,' Jock told Euan. 'You mentioned recently that you and Poppy would be doing your first dance together as a married couple at your wedding reception in the marquee.'

'That's right. Poppy wants us to do that. You know what a great dancer she is.'

'Better than any of us, and she could outdo me at the ceilidh dancing. But she trained in Highland dancing to a level where she considered competing.'

'So what's on your mind?'

'Come in for a moment before we turn into icicles.' Jock beckoned Euan to hurry along and into the bar restaurant.

Euan followed him, glad to feel the warmth of the bar.

The aroma of soup cooking for the lunches wafted through from the kitchen. Jock had staff, but he did a lot of the cooking himself, along with Judy. He'd rustled up the chocolate pudding and only had the chocolate sauce to make nearer lunchtime.

Jock took a deep breath and spoke his mind. 'No offence, Euan, but when it comes to dancing you're not exactly twinkle toes.'

'No,' Euan agreed, 'more like *step on your toes*.'

'And you don't want to do that to Poppy when she's wearing her beautiful wedding dress and all your guests are watching the pair of you waltz for your first dance at your wedding reception.'

'Waltz?' Euan had recently attempted to learn ceilidh dancing under Jock's strict tuition. As had other men. They'd all improved, adding to the success of the ceilidh nights. Now he had to learn to waltz?

'Exactly. I'm sure you can dance not too bad, but that's not good enough when all eyes will be on you leading Poppy around the dance floor.'

Euan's heart sank. 'I don't want to mess this up for her. But I—'

'You need to practise. One or two lessons will make you confident and less likely to muck things up,' Jock advised.

'Dance lessons?'

'Yes, and I'm happy to give you a few tips. The pair of you can waltz around the function room. I'll watch and give you advice. And of course, Poppy will keep you right, but it's always good to have someone instruct you.'

'You'd let us use the function room? We could use one of the rooms in my farmhouse. I could lift the rug in the living room and—'

'No, let me help. I'll even film the two of you. Then you can watch to see where you go right and wrong. After two or three lessons, you can practice at home. But there's nothing quite like waltzing around a proper dance floor. I have great music and I'm a stickler for posture and technique.'

Euan pondered the offer.

Jock shrugged. 'It's up to yourself, Euan. But my offer is genuine. I'll have you waltzing like a pro in jig time.'

Euan's first reaction was to say no. But then he thought about Poppy. 'Okay, thanks, Jock. I'll do it. I'm having lunch with Poppy later. I'm sure she'll be happy to go along with this.'

Jock rubbed his hands together. 'Great. The function room is busy most nights, especially on the run up to Christmas. But it's free most afternoons. We'll sort out a time that suits.'

'Thanks again, Jock.' Euan smiled as he ventured out into the cold day again, picturing himself learning to waltz. It was surely easier than ceilidh dancing, and he'd nearly nailed that. Feeling bolstered and eager to tell Poppy, he headed back up to his farmhouse.

Lochlan saw the figure of Euan in the distance walking through the snow as he stood outside the old farm building he was renovating, making it into a house. The work was almost complete.

He'd bought the property for a fair price due to it needing a lot of work done. As a professional builder he'd torn the structure back to the bone and rebuilt it to create a home for himself — and Kity.

His small building business had thrived, based in one of the nearby towns, but he'd left it in his workers' capable hands and come back to the village to help his uncle. Dougal had sustained an arm injury, and as a local handyman joiner, he couldn't keep up with the work he'd promised.

Dougal was in his fifties and did joinery and building work around the village, for the farmers, fishermen, local trades and businesses, and fixed things in the cottages and houses there and further afield.

Lochlan had stepped in and handled the work, and although Dougal was now fit and fine to work on his own, Lochlan had lingered, hoping to find a way into Kity's heart. And he had. They were dating now. But he was hoping for more than that.

He looked again at Euan, pleased for him that he was soon to marry Poppy. This was the type of happiness he hoped for with Kity.

But first, he had to finish the porch, install a lantern beside the front door, drape fairy lights around the windows and set the scene for what was in his heart. To propose to Kity. Ask her to marry him. He had the ring. He'd checked the necessary paperwork and all the things they had to give notice of if they wanted to get married before Christmas. He was cutting it neat, but it was doable. By his calculations, they could get married a week before Christmas Day. A few days after Euan and Poppy tied the knot.

Kity, a long time ago when they were at school, had said that she loved the winter, and Christmas, and if she ever got married, she wanted to be a December bride.

She'd only been a wee girl, but it seemed like a cherished wish. She said she wanted a beautiful dress, a wonderful cake and the boy of her dreams.

The dress he was sure would be attainable. The ladies of the bee had all helped Poppy, especially Judy and Eila.

Gordon could rustle up a wedding cake. The tea shop cakes were marvellous and Gordon was a first–class baker.

And then he sighed nervously, thinking about her last wish. Hopefully he was the man she'd want to marry. He knew he could make her happy if only she'd let him. The most annoying boy in the entire world had always loved her. He wanted to build a happy life with Kity and not be annoying.

He'd tamed the large garden that surrounded the house, and furnished it with a mix of vintage pieces and modern appliances. Kity loved vintage, second–hand, pre–loved. These were the words she often used when chatting to him about her knitting, crafts and the decor of where she lived above the shop.

The decor had been selected to carefully match the ice cream colours she liked, and when he'd been painting and decorating the rooms, he found that he loved it too. The warm cream in the hallway felt welcoming. The white walls of the living room were offset with touches of soft blues and beige. The kitchen was vanilla. The bathroom pale aquamarine. The lighting consisted of lamps, some with glass shades like Gordon had in his tea shop. Others with traditional floral shades. The spotlights he'd installed highlighted the kitchen and the fairy lights were the last to be hung up for his proposal night.

Kity was attending the bee later, and he still wondered if he should invite her to come to the house after it was finished at around nine. It would depend on how much work he got finished. The snow was an unexpected hindrance and help. Climbing up ladders on snowy, blustery days wasn't smart. But it created the perfect atmosphere for the house all lit up at night with twinkling lights.

Kity knew he was renovating the property either to live in or sell if he moved back to the nearby town. But now that they were dating, he planned to sell his house in the town and stay in the village.

He didn't have Euan's type of wealth, but he did very well for himself.

Since telling her about the house, he'd only shown her the architectural drawings he'd sketched depicting a beautiful house that was a mix of traditional and modern design. He wanted to work on it behind the scenes so he could reveal it when it was finished — and propose to her.

When she'd shown an interest in the progress recently, wondering how his building work was getting on, hinting that she was interested in seeing it, he'd made an excuse. He told her that it wasn't fit for her to step inside, sighting wonky floors, holes in the roof and a shaky structure. According to him there were holes and divots in the rough garden with its untamed grass surrounding the house, so it wasn't suitable for her to stand there either.

She'd taken him at his word and let him get on with it, content to see the house take shape in the distance from the view of the fields out her kitchen window.

Determined to try to get the house ready in time, Lochlan set about finishing the porch, working as the snow fluttered around him and with the wind blowing the cold sea air up from the shore.

41

Strong, tall, fit and hardy, Lochlan tackled the tasks.

He pulled a woollen hat on over his dark hair, wore all–weather warm clothing including a thick winter jacket and steel toe cap boots. He was ready for the elements. There was only one thing in jeopardy. If Kity said no to his proposal, he had nothing to shield himself from a broken heart.

But it was worth the risk he told himself fiercely, hammering the porch into submission in the biting cold. The wind whipped across his pale, handsome features, and his blue eyes blinked away the snow. He loved Kity more than anything. He always had. He always would.

Euan knocked on Poppy's cottage door.

She opened it.

'I won't come in. I just wanted to tell you that Abby and Josh are in Dublin. Minnie says they probably won't be home for Christmas so you'll only have five bridesmaids.'

Poppy absorbed the news. 'Well, Eila has the fabric for Abby's dress on standby, but she hasn't even cut the pattern. We really weren't sure if she'd be away with Josh. They've been jaunting all over the place this past wee while. Good on them. But at least Eila won't have to start making another dress.' She smiled at him. 'Thanks for letting me know. I was scribbling notes in my bridal journal, so now I can tick Abby's dress off the list.'

The snow was becoming heavier.

'I'm heading back to the farmhouse. I've other news to tell you, but I'll explain later. It's fun stuff. Jock has plans for us.'

'Jock?'

Euan nodded and dug into his shopping bag. 'I bought a cake for our lunch. I'll give it to you now. I didn't want you having to bake something.'

'A chocolate Yule log?' She didn't disguise her delight and surprise.

'Gordon's new recipe. Remember to give him feedback later at the bee.'

'I love chocolate cake.'

Euan smiled. 'Don't munch it all. Leave a slice for me.'

Kity laughed. 'You know me too well,' she joked with him.

'I'll be over in the afternoon. Away in and keep warm.'

Striding away, he headed across the field to his farmhouse. Steeped in evergreens and hardy florals, it faced the sea and provided Euan with his favourite view of the seascape. The water sparkled in the dawn light and he was up most mornings early to start his work in the fields. But even on winter nights the vast sky stretched across the seaside and he enjoyed the sense of calm it provided after a busy day.

He missed the farmhouse when he was away travelling to give talks on his flowers, and was always happy to be back. He was a homebody, not a wanderer. And now he looked forward to sharing his home with Poppy.

The farmhouse had large windows that let in plenty of light, and the beige, pale grey and soft gold tones of the decor created a bright and airy atmosphere. Scatter rugs matching the colour scheme were on the polished wooden floors, and table lamps created a warm and welcoming glow.

Kicking the snow from his boots, he stepped inside and took the shopping through to the kitchen that extended to the dining room. He tended to eat his meals alone in the cosy kitchen using the sturdy wooden table as a second desk. This routine would probably change once Poppy moved in, though usually when she came over to the farmhouse for dinner they both ate their meals in the kitchen.

The shortbread, minus one piece, refilled the biscuit tin, and he put the kettle on for a cup of tea while he munched the sugar sprinkled wedge of shortbread.

While the kettle boiled, he hung his jacket in the hall and went to have a look at the improvements Pearl had made.

'Impressive,' he mumbled to himself, seeing the little touches she'd added here and there throughout the house.

Opening the wardrobe, he saw the padded hangers ready for Poppy's clothes, and a rush of excitement charged through him. Soon they'd be sharing the farmhouse, sharing their lives together. Sometimes the waves of happiness took him aback.

He closed the wardrobe doors and glanced at the quilt on his double bed. A new quilt was no doubt in the making. Perhaps even being worked on that night at the bee without Poppy knowing that their sewing included gifts for their wedding.

But he knew nothing, he reminded himself. And neither would Poppy. At least not from his lips.

Heading downstairs to his study, he noticed that Pearl hadn't interfered with his work. A solid oak desk that was older than the farmhouse stood in the heart of the room, and in contrast, his computer was cutting edge, silver grey and stylish. Business documents were stored in antique cabinets. Pearl had polished the shiny veneers so they reflected his study like glass, but everything else wasn't fussed with thankfully.

Euan sat down at his desk facing his much–loved view of the fields and the sea.

He saw Poppy's cottage out the window. It looked so pretty covered in snow.

Poppy intended to keep the cottage as her business, while moving into the farmhouse with him. The best of both worlds.

Embroidery Cottage was something he didn't want to lease out to anyone else, even though Poppy hadn't taken it for granted that she'd continue using it even though there was a spare room in the farmhouse she could work from. He wanted her to have the cottage.

Noticing something shimmer, he squinted out the window through the snow. Far in the distance, in one of the fields beyond the cottage, he saw lights flickering in the old farmhouse building that Lochlan was restoring.

Euan frowned. Yes, it was snowing, but it was a bit early for Christmas lights and decorations. Mind you, he'd just given Poppy a Yule log.

Shrugging off his suspicions, he went through to the kitchen to make the tea and get a bit of work done before his late lunch date.

Eila braved the snow and hurried from her dress shop along to the tea shop for lunch.

She wore a warm jacket and a white woolly hat, but the wind blew through the strands of her long blonde hair, and she put a spurt on to get out of the cold.

Gordon was working in the kitchen when she bustled in, windblown but smiling at him. She looked so beautiful. The first time he'd met her in her dress shop, he was sure he'd fallen a little in love. Now he loved her completely, and they were hopefully getting married in the not too distant future. Eila had said she wanted to be a spring bride.

She planted a kiss on his cheek and adjusted his chef's hat as she'd knocked it askew in her enthusiasm.

He grinned at her. 'Hello there, trouble.'

It was their usual routine that on certain days Eila would pop along to have lunch or dinner in the tea shop kitchen with Gordon if he wasn't too busy. Those times were rare, but at least she could chat to him while he worked and she ate her meals.

While she hung up her jacket and stuffed her hat into one of the pockets, he served up a bowl of Scotch broth.

Eila settled herself at the little kitchen table tucked into the corner where Gordon ate his meals and where she was always welcome.

'It's freezing outside,' she said. 'I saw the snow, but...brrrrrh! I didn't think it would be so bone–chilling.'

'Get that hot soup down you.' He cut two slices of crusty bread, put them on a plate with a side portion of green salad and served that up to her.

'Thanks, Gordon. This is just what I need. No one makes better soup than you.'

'You're just saying that because it's true,' he joked with her.

Eila laughed and ate a chunk of bread before tucking into her broth. 'Mmmm,' she mumbled, smiling at him.

He stirred a pot of butterscotch sauce. 'I have gossip, but I don't know whether to tell you or let you hear it at the bee tonight.'

'No, spill,' Eila insisted.

'Pearl popped in for scones and she said that Minnie had news from Abby.'

'What news?' Eila said eagerly.

'Josh has whisked them off to Dublin. They're spending Christmas there, probably.'

'So Abby won't be a bridesmaid at Poppy's wedding,' she wanted to confirm.

'I don't think so. But talk to Minnie. She has all the news.'

'I'll do that. I was happy to make a last minute dress if Abby needed it, but if she's in Dublin I won't have to. But I need to talk to Kity about her dress. She needs to come in for a fitting.'

'Kity will be at the bee so you can tell her this evening.'

'I will. Poppy has organised the wedding plans so well. I don't want to mess things up by not having all the dresses sewn for the bridesmaids.'

'You won't. You're a whiz with that sewing machine of yours.'

Eila blushed at the compliment. 'You think so?'

'Yes, and I've seen the lovely bridesmaid dress you've made for the wedding. You'll make a great job of Kity's dress too.'

Eila smiled at Gordon and felt the warmth in her heart for him more every day. He was the sweetest man in the world. In her world. He backed her up on everything, something no one else had ever done. It made her feel that she could take a chance on things, expand her dress designs, safe in the knowledge that Gordon wouldn't flatten her enthusiasm.

He poured two cups of tea. One for her, one for himself. 'What are you grinning at?'

'At you, silly.'

'Can we have our crumpets heated, Gordon?' a customer called into the kitchen.

'Yes, I'll zap them before I pour the hot butterscotch sauce on them,' Gordon said, sounding as if this was no bother at all.

'Thanks, Gordon.' The customer, one of the local farmers, disappeared back to his table at the front of the tea shop to join three other hungry farmers who were in for their lunch. A treat on a cold day.

The snow had taken a lot of people off guard, arriving in a freezing flurry and putting everyone in the notion of something warm for lunch. The jam roly–poly and hot custard had been gone in a flash, so he used the crumpets as back–up.

'Hot crumpet,' Eila teased him. 'I didn't know that was on the menu today.'

'Rascal,' Gordon scolded her playfully. 'Where's the shy young lady who arrived here to open her dress shop and kept herself to herself for ages before becoming part of the community?'

'Oh, she's long gone. If she was ever really here.'

Gordon prepared the crumpets efficiently, and as he passed by Eila he gave her a kiss. 'I'm glad to hear it.'

And off he went, through to the serve the customers their lunch, leaving Eila to eat her soup and bread — and plan what she was going to take with her to the bee that evening.

Her dress shop stocked rolls of fabric and thread. When she made dresses from cotton, often floral prints or polka dots, she tied the off–cuts into neat bundles and gave them to the ladies at the bee for making quilts.

She'd been making a few orders for classic tea dresses in lovely cottons, and had several little handy bundles put aside. Minnie and Pearl had been working on the wedding quilt for Poppy and Euan, and she'd heard that all it needed was the binding stitched on and it was finished. So as not to let Poppy see it, or any of the other quilted items the members were making as wedding gifts, the ladies had been doing secret sewing in their houses. Eila had been so busy making the dresses for the bridesmaids and running her shop that she hadn't gone along to any of the secret sewing, but

Minnie had promised she'd take pictures of the wedding quilt and give her a sneak peek at the bee when Poppy wasn't looking.

Eila loved the bee nights and living by the sea in the accommodation at the back of her dress shop. It was so handy to live and work in such a lovely location and she didn't miss her life in Glasgow. Like a few others, she was in her early thirties and moved away from the city to the coastal village where she'd thrived personally and professionally. Finding love with Gordon was more than she'd ever hoped for, and she'd always loved dressmaking.

After finishing her soup, she heard Gordon still chatting to customers at the front of the shop and serving people who came in to buy his bakery items and confectionery.

On a cake stand that Gordon had been loading with cakes and scones, she eyed a strawberry pink fairy cake.

She was just about to steal it and confess later, when Gordon walked in and pointed at her.

'Caught! Scoundrel.' He laughed, unable to scold her seriously.

'It was just too tempting.'

Gordon gave her the cake. 'Be tempted.'

Topping up her cup with more tea, they chatted while he continued cooking and she consumed a slice of the profits. But no one could be happier about that than Gordon.

CHAPTER FOUR

Jock wrapped his arms around Judy and hugged her as she worked at the computer in the small office area of the bar restaurant's kitchen. 'What are you up to?'

'I'm updating the bee's website. A few members have emailed new items they're selling. I've almost finished. They've written the blurb and sent the pictures, so I'm just adding them to the items for sale.' Judy showed him the orders they'd had recently. 'Customers are buying items and then coming back for more. Sales of quilts and knitted items for the winter are rising so it's been worthwhile having a website for the bee.'

'I'm pleased to hear it,' he said. Then he peered at a couple of party dresses that were listed. 'Are those your handiwork?'

'They are. My wee cocktail dress was snapped up, and an evening dress. I'll get them wrapped up and take them to the post office later.'

'I'll take them for you. I've business correspondence to post.'

Judy smiled round at him.

Jock gave her another squeeze and then got on with the cooking, preparing a stew with lots of fresh vegetables.

'I think it's a great idea to let Euan try waltzing with Poppy,' she said, finishing the updates.

'Euan looked a bit dubious at first, but then he realised it would be handy to learn before the wedding.'

'I remember our first dance.'

Jock put the pot down, started to hum the song they'd chosen for their waltz, walked over and pulled Judy gently into hold. Giggling while he sang to her, they danced around the kitchen and finished with him dipping her.

'I've a big bag of tatties from the farm,' a man said, walking in loaded with the potatoes. 'Where do you want me to put them?'

'Over there beside the vegetable rack please,' said Jock, straightening up as if he hadn't been dipping his wife.

The farmer couldn't contain quipping as he walked away. 'Nice to see that you two are still canoodling after all these years together.'

'Aye,' said Jock. 'And they said we'd never last.'

'The naysayers got that wrong, didn't they?' Judy chirped.

Jock smiled at her. 'Accusing us of marrying in haste. The cheek of them.'

'It's not how long you know someone, it's how much you love them.'

Jock pulled Judy into his arms again. 'I knew the first night I met you that you were the girl for me. We were dancing then.'

'And dancing now.'

Continuing where they'd left off, Jock and Judy waltzed playfully in the kitchen.

Poppy put the pie in the oven to heat and got the plates and cutlery ready for her lunch with Euan.

The kitchen decor was white and blue and it had an old–fashioned wooden dresser that was painted eggshell blue. Poppy loved the decor and the little touches such as the ceramic teapots that matched the theme.

The white lace curtains were tied back with blue ribbons, and she looked out at the back garden that was covered in snow. The urge to run out and build a snowman was doused when a message came through from Euan that he would be there in fifteen minutes. Even Poppy with all her enthusiasm couldn't build a snowman that fast. But the thought was nice.

With the pie heating and the kettle set to boil, she went through to the spare bedroom that she used for storing her work and stock. It was kitted out with a wardrobe, chest of drawers and a large table for cutting fabric and packing the orders. The wardrobe and drawers were filled with her fabric stash, boxes of embroidery thread and other sewing items. Her artwork and cutting equipment were stored there too. In one of the drawers all her inked illustrations for her patterns were kept in folders.

Again, she looked out at the snow. The cottage's thick stone walls shielded it from the sound of the wind whipping across the fields. It was something else she loved about living at the cottage, the quietude. In the city the hustle and bustle sounded loud and clear, even the low buzz of it at night. But here...the quiet atmosphere was calming.

Euan had assured her that if it snowed, she'd never be snowed–in when she was at the cottage. But that didn't sound too bad, as long as Euan was there with her.

Blinking away her scattered thoughts, she quickly selected skeins of stranded cotton embroidery thread that she needed for later, added them to her sewing box in the living room, and then hurried through to the kitchen to check on the lunch.

A loud knock on the front door announced Euan's arrival.

'I'm in the kitchen,' she called through to him.

He took his boots off in the hallway as they were coated with snow, hung his jacket up, and then padded through to the kitchen in his thick wool socks. Even without his boots, his six foot plus stature towered over her as he gave her a kiss.

'I've put a load of logs and kindling in the storage rack outside,' he said.

'I appreciate it. I love having a real log fire.'

He washed his hands at the sink. 'The pie smells tasty.' He glanced around. 'What can I do to help?'

'Make the tea please. The kettle should be boiled.'

While Euan made the tea, Poppy served up the pie that had plenty of vegetables including carrots, turnip and potatoes in a rich savoury gravy.

'Help yourself to the bread,' she told him.

He did, buttering a slice of it and tucking in. 'I'm ready for this. I've only had a cuppa and a piece of shortbread.'

'You'll need more to fuel you up in cold weather like this.'

'A load of orders from my buyers came in for the holly and other evergreens, so I'll tackle those after I have lunch with you.' He grinned. 'Topped up on pie.'

'Remember to keep some holly for the marquee's decor,' she reminded him.

'I've got a whole niche set aside for everything we need. Are you sure you don't want me to order you out of season flowers for your bridal bouquet?'

'No, I'm trusting you to make something from whatever the winter has to spare. It'll add to the authenticity of being a Christmas bride.'

Euan glanced out at the snowscape. 'A snow bride. I've seen snowfall like this in other years and I think we're definitely in for a whiteout Christmas.'

'That sounds perfect.'

Euan smiled over at her as they sat at the kitchen table eating their lunch. 'It does, doesn't it.' Any doubts he had that the cold could scupper their plans faded.

'A snow bride.' Poppy tilted her head and tried out the new phrase. 'I like the sound of that.'

'The white ribbons you wanted for your bridal bouquet arrived. I ordered plenty, along with pale pink for the bridesmaids.' He dug into his pocket. 'I cut a couple of samples. I thought you'd like to see them.'

Poppy put down her cutlery and admired the ribbons. 'These are exactly what I had in mind.'

'I ordered two widths so that I can vary them when I make the bouquets. The thinner ribbons will trail well, but I'll wrap the flower stems secure with the broader ribbons.'

'I love that the groom is creating the bouquets.' She smiled across the table at him as she continued to eat her lunch.

'I learned when I was younger and it's something I enjoy making. I've actually made wedding bouquets before for local couples, but they were summer weddings. The winter is a challenge, but there's a beauty to the florals and foliage at this time of year. I promise I'll make something beautiful for you and the bridesmaids.'

'I know you will, Euan. And a buttonhole for your suit.'

'I'll make it to match in with the theme. And are you certain you don't want me to wear a kilt?'

'As much as you look handsome in a kilt, we both know that you're more comfortable wearing a suit.'

This was true. 'And it's a bespoke suit.'

When Sholto heard that Euan was getting married, he was the first one to offer to make him a suit. The other large mansion on the hill that lay vacant for months at a time belonged to the wealthy and successful Sholto. He owned a top tailoring company in Edinburgh. His two sons, Hamish and Fraser, were around the same age as Euan. Cairn, Sholto's assistant, in his thirties, was part of the family's rich tailoring business.

Cairn was like a son to Sholto, and the four men caused ructions whenever they came down from the city to stay at the big house.

Renowned as some of the most handsome men around, they were four heartbreakers, and a couple of them had shown an interest in Eila and Kity earlier in the year.

Romance didn't work out for Cairn or Hamish with the local lassies, but friendships were formed, old grievances aired and mended, and Euan had gone up to Edinburgh for the day to be fitted out with a classic suit for his wedding. It was now hanging in his wardrobe.

Sholto had insisted on kitting Euan out with a shirt, tie, shoes, everything for a total bespoke look, and wouldn't accept payment. This was his gift to Euan.

Although Sholto and the others had planned to come back for a visit before Christmas, this plan got scuppered when they were once again hired to create the suits for a television series. So they wouldn't be attending the wedding even though they'd been invited.

Poppy cleared their plates away and cut two slices of the chocolate Yule log. 'There was something else you were going to tell me.'

'Yes, Jock's offered to teach me to waltz so I won't give you a showing up for our first dance at the wedding reception.' He explained the details. 'I said, yes. I hope you agree.'

'I do, that sounds like fun. You know I love to dance and it'll be great to have the function room to ourselves to practise on.'

'Jock says we'll arrange suitable days, in the afternoons.'

'That works for me. We'll have to decide on a song we both like, or one that means something special to us.'

Euan couldn't think of one. 'Jock has a great selection of music. I'm sure we'll find something we both like.'

'I want to add this to my wedding notes.' She sounded excited.

While Poppy ran through to pick up her folder from the living room, Euan tucked into the Yule log.

She came back with the folder, opened it and scribbled notes.

Euan smiled over at her, but she didn't see him as she concentrated on adding whatever it was she was jotting down about the dancing and the music.

Closing the folder and putting it aside on the table, she sampled the cake, and nodded. 'This is sooo rich with chocolate.'

'Tell Gordon when you see him at the tea shop tonight that his new recipe gets a big thumbs up from me.'

'And me,' Poppy chimed–in.

Enjoying their cake and tea, they chatted about other plans for their wedding before Euan headed out into the snow to get on with his work.

Kity had unpacked all the new yarn and tackled the online orders for the Christmas selection and knitting patterns.

The shelves in the shop were filled with a wonderful range of yarns, and the carousels were restocked with patterns, knitting needles, crochet hooks and other handy accessories.

Lochlan had put new shelves up, replacing the wonky old ones. That's how they'd become reacquainted — Lochlan had arrived one autumn day to do the repair work that Dougal had arranged with Kity. She'd been up a ladder outside her shop hanging up bunting, and had been so taken aback when Lochlan spoke up to her that she'd tumbled and fallen from the ladder straight into his strong arms. And from there she'd found herself falling in love with him.

With the snow still sprinkling down outside, she hadn't stopped for lunch and had continued to work until the late afternoon light began to fade.

The orders were piled in the room at the back of the shop that led out to her garden. The shed had become her little haven, and she'd made curtains for the windows, and set up a comfy chair and table that she used for knitting and other crafts.

Peeking out the back window, she wondered if she'd need to get a heater for the shed. It always felt cosy, but now that it was iced white, maybe a bit of heat would be needed. She'd put a rug down on the floor and she could easily add a blanket to her chair to wrap around her while she was knitting or practising her sewing. Although she didn't especially need the shed, she liked it. Perhaps Lochlan could advise her.

She'd been watching his house in the distance and was sure she'd seen flickering lights. But when she'd blinked, they were gone. It was probably just the glare from the whiteout across the fields. The hedgerows bordering the fields looked like someone had shaken icing sugar over them. The trees were iced white too, creating a picturesque view that she would've lingered over if she hadn't needed to get on with her work.

The last task before she had to take the orders to the post office was the window display.

It wasn't Christmas but...the Christmas yarns were selling well, so she decided to compromise. Selecting white yarn, from double knitting to lace weight and chunky, she made that the basis of the display. Then she added rich reds, soft greens and touches of silvery grey.

Braving the snow, she ran outside to view the display, ran back in and adjusted a couple of balls and skeins, then draped clear twinkle lights along the edges of the window.

Satisfied with her handiwork, she put on her jacket, a woolly hat, and took the parcels to the post office.

Gusts of wind swept in from the sea, but she hurried along the esplanade and darted inside the post office.

Dropping the parcels off, she ventured out into the snow again, feeling it beneath her boots. It had hardly stopped snowing all day.

Breathing in the fresh sea air, she relished the energy of the elements, and it made her knitting shop feel extra cosy when she hurried back inside and closed the door against the icy day.

She took her jacket and hat off and checked that the pink jumper and cardigan for Eila were finished properly. She planned to go along to the bee a little bit earlier than usual so she could give Gordon the knitwear before Eila arrived.

Gordon had to bake another batch of fairy cakes. Customers enjoyed the ones he had on offer and there were none left for the bee members. He'd promised to let the members sample the new recipe, especially as the cakes were going to be part of the wedding buffet.

Rustling up the pink icing, he made sure the cakes had cooled on a rack before smoothing the topping on them and adding pink sprinkles.

As it was such a cold day, he changed the evening menu for the tea shop and included winter stew and mashed potatoes. The stew smelled so tasty while it was cooking on the stove that he knew what he was having for his dinner.

The tea shop had been busy all day. Sometimes there was a lull, but not today. And farmers had booked a table near the window in advance for the evening. They were celebrating the arrival of one of the farmer's sons. He was home for a holiday and they'd decided to have a meal out. So the busy day was set to stretch into a busy evening, but Gordon was in his element when the tea shop was popular. He enjoyed the buzz of it.

Lochlan fitted the lantern on the outside of the house beside the front door. It was one of those traditional vintage–style lanterns that he thought suited the exterior of the property.

The porch was finished quicker than he'd anticipated, so it left plenty of time to tackle another task he'd been working on — the fairy lights. He'd draped the outdoor version around the door and windows. Inside, he'd decorated the living room with lights.

A roaring log fire burned in the hearth and the scent of the fresh cut logs made the house feel like home. Warm. Welcoming. Somewhere to snuggle up by the fireside. Toast marshmallows. Watch Christmas films. All those seasonal things.

He'd painted the walls white and used colour accents, like the sky blue painted alcove in the hallway lit with a glass shaded lamp. Glass lamps were his favourite as they created such wonderful patches of glowing colour through a house.

Wall lights were dotted around in strategic places, and every niche in the rooms had a lamp or lighting to bestow a cosy atmosphere.

The two bedrooms, both with double beds, featured built–in wardrobes and antique pieces. Traditional and modern. He'd bought quilts from the bee members for the beds and the sofa in the living room. The ladies assumed they were for Dougal's house. He didn't correct them.

The large living room stretched the full length of the house with a dining area and open plan lounge. Windows offered a panoramic view of the sea on one side and the hills and forest on the other. The middle of the living room could be easily cleared to create a dancing area for parties. Entertaining guests was an integral part of village life, and apart from the party nights at the bar restaurant, and village events celebrated in marquees in the fields, local people invited friends to their cottages and houses. Lochlan wanted that too, and with having so much space to play around with, he'd built in a floor area that could double as a dance floor.

Throughout the day, he kept glancing over at the back view of Kity's knitting shop. A light shone from the kitchen window upstairs as the day darkened, and the glow from the front shop shone through to the back window on the ground floor.

It spurred him on, knowing Kity was over there, and that he would see her later that evening. The house was ready.

He checked the ring, opening the velvet box and watching the white fire of the solitaire diamond dance in the white gold setting. He closed it again and put it aside safely. He was surely going to wear out the lustre by his constant checking of it.

The time was ticking in. He needed to call Kity and set up his plan.

Kity was putting the jumper and cardigan in a bag when her phone rang. She smiled when she saw the caller.

'Hello, stranger,' she chirped.

'I know you're off to the tea shop for the bee tonight, but it usually finishes around nine.'

'That's right.' She wondered if he wanted to walk her home. Even though her knitting shop was a minute's walk from the tea shop, Lochlan liked to turn up some evenings to walk back with her. Often she'd invite him in for tea, and they'd snuggle for a while upstairs in the living room before he headed home to Dougal's house.

'I was wondering if you'd be up for a peek at the house.'

'You've finished it?' She could barely contain her excitement.

'Yes, so would you like to come over for the grand tour?'

'I'd love to.'

'I'll pick you up at the tea shop. Message me when you're about to finish and I'll come down.'

Looking forward to seeing the new house later, and Lochlan, Kity got her things ready to head to the bee, including her craft bag with her knitting and sewing in it.

She'd added something extra with the jumper and cardigan — a pink tea cosy she'd knitted to promote the new yarn. It had been in the window display, but now that she'd changed the pink hues to winter tones, she didn't need it. Usually, she'd sell promo items on her website, but she thought she'd give it to Gordon for his tea shop.

The snow had called a truce just before Kity wrapped up warm and headed out to the bee. The gusts of wind were gone too, creating a crisp, fresh feeling to the night air. She could even hear her boots crunch through the snow as she walked along.

The glow from the tea shop shone out on to the blanket of white, making it look so welcoming. The new pink canopy added to the warm glow of the lanterns. If the tea shop looked this pretty now, she could only imagine what it would look like once it was decorated with Christmas lights.

CHAPTER FIVE

'You're early,' Gordon chirped, smiling at Kity as she walked in.

She held up the bag and gave him a knowing look.

'Oh, yes, come away through to the kitchen.'

She followed him, noting that none of the bee members had arrived and that the function room at the back was empty. The tea shop itself was busy with every table taken. Keyed up to give Gordon the jumper and cardigan without Eila finding out, the faces of the customers didn't register with her. She doubted Eila would be early for the bee as she was usually the tail end member. But there was every chance that Eila would breeze in to see Gordon and scupper her plan to give the items to him.

Fortunately, the latter didn't happen, and Kity handed the bag to Gordon in the kitchen without anyone else seeing what they were up to.

Gordon peered in the bag but didn't lift the items out. 'These look beautiful. Thank you so much for doing this, Kity.'

'There's a wee extra in there too, for your tea shop.'

Gordon carefully rummaged in the bag and pulled out the cosy. 'I'll buy this too.'

'No, it was part of my display. Take it. I thought it would match your pink decor.'

'That's so kind of you. Here, have a pink fairy cake.'

Kity was glad to be plied with the tasty treat. She took a bite. 'This is yummy.'

'I've tweaked the recipe specially for the wedding reception buffet. There's a dash of champagne in the cake mix.'

'Really?' Kity took another bite and nodded.

Gordon tucked the bag with the jumper and cardigan in the cupboard where he kept his clean aprons, but he held the tea cosy in his clutches.

He'd just stashed the bag and closed the cupboard door when Eila walked in, smiling.

'Am I late for the bee?' said Eila. She'd just stopped by to see Gordon and hadn't expected to see Kity there.

'No, I'm early,' Kity explained. 'I wanted to make a start on my knitting and popped along while the snow had stopped.'

'Look what Kity gave me.' He showed Eila the tea cosy.

'It was part of my window display, but I've changed the theme, so I thought Gordon could make use of it,' Kity blathered, trying not to sound relieved that they'd pulled off their plan by a whisker.

'I'm going to put it on one of the vintage teapots,' he said.

'Okay, I'm away through to cast on my stitches,' said Kity. 'I'm working on one of the bridesmaids' bolero patterns.'

Kity was in such a rush to leave that she didn't notice the man standing in the doorway of the kitchen.

Walking into a firm wall of muscle, she stopped when her hand touched his chest. 'Oh, sorry.' She looked and sounded flustered, especially when she saw the intensely good looking man, similar in age and height to Lochlan, smiling down at her. He'd seen her when she'd walked into the tea shop and had decided to talk to her, having admired her from afar.

'Have you got a moment, Kity?' His deep voice resonated through her.

She blinked. He knew her name? She'd didn't know him, but he seemed to know her.

'I've seen you around. You opened the knitting shop and I noticed you went swimming in the sea,' he explained.

Kity's wide–eyed expression indicated she hadn't noticed him.

He took a steadying breath. 'I, eh, was wondering if you're going to any of the party and ceilidh nights at the bar restaurant. And would you like to go with me?'

'I have a boyfriend,' she told him politely, taken aback by his offer. 'I'm dating Lochlan.'

He glanced at her ring finger. 'I know, but you're not officially tied to him.'

By now, Gordon and Eila were glancing at each other concerned about Kity being chatted up, even though it was done politely.

Gordon whispered to Eila. 'Do you think I should tell Lochlan, or not interfere?'

'If you were Lochlan, would you want to know?' said Eila.

Gordon took his phone from his pocket and called Lochlan. He'd done repair work on the tea shop and Gordon had his number. Stepping aside so that the farmer didn't hear him he told Lochlan what was happening.

'One of the farmers is making a play for Kity in the tea shop.'

Lochlan sparked into action. 'I'm on my way.'

'No, I'm keeping an eye on things, so is Eila.' As he was talking to Lochlan, Judy breezed in.

'Jock said you were running short of cheddar cheese. Here's a spare block from our stock.' Judy handed it to Gordon.

Gordon's reaction alerted Judy that something was amiss, and Eila motioned to the farmer still chatting to Kity and the mention again that she had a boyfriend.

Judy cottoned on to what was going on, and hearing the farmer flirting with Kity she stepped into the fray.

'Kity told you that she has a boyfriend,' Judy told him firmly.

His broad shoulders slumped. 'Yes, but—'

'Yes but nothing,' Judy cut–in. 'It's not appropriate for you to be asking her out on a date.'

He backed down from any further comments, nodded and went through to the front of the tea shop and sat down with the other farmers.

As this happened, Minnie and Pearl had walked in and heard the gist of the situation.

The ladies circled around Kity, chatting and sweeping her through to the function room.

Lochlan was still on the phone and could hear what was going on.

'Everything's fine now,' Gordon assured him. 'Judy told him firmly that his interest wasn't wanted.

And Minnie and Pearl have just arrived. If he steps out of line again Minnie will knit his balls for breakfast.'

Lochlan almost smiled. 'Thanks for that, Gordon.' He paused for a second and then said, 'Can you keep a secret?'

'Yes,' said Gordon, stepping further away into the kitchen so no one could overhear. 'What is it?'

'I'm planning to ask Kity to marry me tonight. I've finished the work on the house, and I've set up lights and everything to make it romantic.'

Gordon could hear the trepidation in his tone. 'Don't let this incident put you off your plans.'

'If anything, it's made me even more sure that I want to propose, to let Kity know that I want us to be a couple, to build a future together.'

'Stick to your plan. Everything's fine here now.'

'Thanks again, Gordon, and to Judy and the ladies. I'm coming down to pick Kity up around nine, after the bee finishes and take her back to the house.'

Voices sounded from customers looking for their orders. 'Good luck, not that you'll need it. Kity thinks the world of you.'

'Cheers, Gordon. I can hear you're busy, so I'll let you get on.'

After the call, Gordon started rustling up the orders at speed, grateful for the spare cheddar cheese that Judy had brought. The bar restaurant and the tea shop often helped each other when either of them ran out of items for their business.

He looked to see where Eila had gone, but she'd fetched her craft bag from upstairs and was chatting happily to the other members as the ladies got ready for their knitting and sewing.

Pearl and Minnie set up the sewing machines and others arranged the tables and chairs to suit what they were working on.

Poppy had arrived armed with her embroidery work and her wedding folder. She often shared her latest embroidery patterns with the members and handed out copies of the winter cottage design to anyone wanting to embroider it.

Poppy had agreed that if she saw any hint of secret sewing for things that were maybe part of the gifts some members were working on, she was to avert her eyes. As Poppy was engrossed in planning the wedding items, especially the favours that the ladies were making, she barely noticed what they were up to.

Fabric for the bags being stitched for the favours was handed around, and others divided the necessary tasks to those that preferred to quilt, sew or knit them.

Kity showed Poppy the floral embroidery she'd been satin stitching recently in a small hoop, and asked for tips on ways to perfect her French knots. While Poppy showed Kity her technique, others listened and watched to see how Poppy wrapped the stranded cotton embroidery thread around the needle to create the neat knots. Kity was keen to accept a copy of the winter cottage pattern, and Poppy advised her on how to transfer the pattern on to cotton fabric.

Putting the embroidery aside to continue it at home, Kity worked on knitting the pale pink boleros for the bridesmaids. Minnie and Pearl were knitting their own, but she said she'd knit one for Judy and

Eila. She'd already finished hers and had brought it along with her to show the other ladies. Taking off her cardigan, she put it on over her top to let Poppy and the others see how pretty it looked.

'It's lovely,' said Poppy.

Eila held up a sample of the oyster pink fabric for the bridesmaids' dresses. 'The yarn is such a perfect match.'

Kity dug into her bag and brought out the carefully folded bolero she'd finished knitting. She handed it to Judy. 'This is yours.'

Judy was delighted and tried it on. 'It feels so nice. I'll be wearing this in the bar restaurant long after the wedding. Thank you for knitting it.'

Kity took her bolero off and gave it to Eila to try on for size. 'I'm knitting yours now, but I think you're the same size as me.'

Eila put it on over her blouse and gave them a twirl. 'How does it look?'

She ran her hand gently over the soft yarn and agreed with Judy. 'It really does feel nice and soft and cosy.'

Kity checked the fit. 'Yes, I'll knit yours the same as mine.'

Eila handed it back to Kity and she tucked it safely in her craft bag, then continued knitting the third bolero which was for Eila. Kity was a fast knitter and worked the rows while they chatted about the drawstring bags being made for the favours.

Pearl had a pile of quilted wedding coasters that she was stitching using floral and cotton fabric in shades of pink.

Minnie studied one of the packets of seeds for the favours. 'What seeds are included in the mix?'

'It's Euan's personal selection of seeds for a mix of flowers,' Poppy told Minnie. 'He's printed out these little notes that list the types of seeds and when and how to plant them.' Poppy had the notes tucked in one of the pockets of her folder and put them on the table. 'We'll add a note to each bag.'

Minnie lifted a note and read out some of the flowers listed. 'Cornflowers, pansies, cosmos...I'll definitely try planting these.'

Gordon came through with the tea trolley loaded with round one of cake, scones, his chocolate confectionery, and savoury snacks. 'Help yourselves. And let me know what you think of the pink fairy cakes. They're a new recipe I'm trying out for the wedding buffet.'

Eager to taste the cakes, the members started to put their sewing and knitting aside to enjoy their tea.

'I'll chat to you later about the wedding cake,' Poppy told Gordon. 'When you're less busy.' She could see that the tea shop was buzzing and intended talking to him at the end of the evening. 'But I loved your new recipe Yule log. Euan and I had it for lunch and it's so rich in chocolate.'

Gordon beamed. 'I'm glad you liked it. And yes, we'll chat later about your wedding cake.'

'Are those pictures of the wedding cake you're planning to have?' Minnie leaned over to peek at Poppy's folder that she'd laid open on the table.

'Yes, I cut these from some of the bridal magazines I bought from your shop. And thanks for ordering in the latest copies. I showed them to Gordon a few days ago to give him an idea what I have in mind, and he's done these sketches for the wedding cake with our own personal touches.' She let Minnie see the drawings.

'It'll be a beautiful cake,' Minnie said, admiring the designs.

'Three tiers of cake, iced white, with pink and white fondant roses.' The delight sounded clear in Poppy's voice.

As the evening continued, the members chatted while working on their quilting, embroidery and knitting, and Gordon brought them another round of tea.

Heading back through to the kitchen, he heard Kity tell them about Lochlan. 'He's finished the house he was restoring, and picking me up here after the bee to take me up for the grand tour. I've been eager to see his handiwork.'

Gordon smiled to himself and kept Lochlan's proposal plan a secret. It was clear from Kity's tone that she'd no idea what he had in mind later that night.

Poppy ate one of the fairy cakes with her tea. 'Gordon says there's champagne in this recipe. They'll be ideal for the buffet.'

Kity popped a square of sweet Scottish tablet in her mouth and nodded as she continued knitting Eila's bolero. 'Gordon's tablet is delicious too,' she mumbled.

Poppy checked her notes. She was making great progress. 'Thanks for all your help with my wedding plans.'

The ladies smiled, pleased to be part of the excitement.

Pearl was happy quilting the coasters. 'I enjoy sewing with a purpose. I know a lot of us sell the things we make, but I like quilting wee things like these coasters.'

'I like that you've included crafts as part of your wedding theme,' said Kity.

'We wanted to have things that represented both of us — my embroidery and Euan's flowers, so that's why we selected those for the main favours,' Poppy explained. 'Then I realised that crafts were such an integral part of our life here, especially our bee nights. The quilted, knitted and hand crafted items then became part of the wedding reception plan and now I'm so pleased seeing them take shape.'

'We'll need another wedding soon so that we can enjoy more of this,' said Pearl.

The other members agreed.

'You and Gordon,' Judy suggested to Eila.

Eila shook her head. 'We've no firm date, but maybe the spring or summer. It'll be a wee while yet before we start planning.'

The conversation included the latest news about Abby and Josh.

'They're in Dublin,' Minnie told the ladies and held up her phone to show them the pictures. 'I know we thought there was a chance they'd be married at Christmas, but I don't think they'll be back here for any of the festive season.'

'Abby says they're getting married in the New Year, so we've that to look forward to,' Pearl enthused.

'Remember, we've got our sewing and mending evening here in a couple of nights,' Minnie reminded them.

Once a month they held an extra bee night that concentrated on all sorts of mending, whether it was adding patches to jackets or jeans, repairing items that were well–loved but worn, and jumpers and other knitted items that could be mended if they had holes in them or were frayed. They'd been keen to share their tips on visible mending as well as techniques that repaired items without the stitches being shown. In contrast, the visible mending was part of the design, bright coloured threads used to make patches and the stitching became a creative element of the repair.

One of the members held up the dress she was altering for the wedding. Not a bridesmaid, but one of the guests, she'd decided to upscale a fifties tea dress and make it suitable for wearing to the wedding.

'I've taken such an interest in sewing and mending,' the woman said, showing them the floral motif she'd embroidered on the front of the dress to cover a small stain.

'It's a lovely dress,' Judy commented. 'Wearing vintage feels great and there are so many pre–loved bargains to be had these days.'

'I picked this up for sweetie money,' the woman told them. 'A real bargain. There was only a little bit of wear and a minor stain. I snapped it up and now look at it. The repairs are fun to stitch and the quality of the design feels great when I'm wearing it.'

Another member spoke up, encouraged by what she'd seen. 'I must have a rummage through my wardrobe. There are dresses I've discarded for ages hanging in it. Seeing what you've done with your tea dress makes me want to give it a go.'

'You should,' Minnie encouraged her. 'Bring it along to the sewing and mending night and we'll help you with ideas.'

'I'll pop along too,' said Kity. 'If anyone has a knitted jumper or cardigan that's seen better days, bring it and I'll show you how to repair it.'

Several members were eager to take Kity up on her offer especially as winter brought out everyone's winter woollies that hadn't been worn for a while.

'If you have a darning mushroom, bring it along with you,' Kity added. 'It makes the repairs easier, but I'll bring a couple you can use if you don't have one.'

With their plans for the forthcoming sewing and mending night made, they continued to chat and work on their crafts.

Gordon brought a trolley through to them with cups of hot chocolate. 'It's such a cold night, I thought you'd all like a cup to heat you up before you head home.'

'Hot chocolate!' Eila was the first to accept. 'Yes, please.'

All of them were happy to accept and thanked Gordon.

'Help yourselves to the marshmallows,' he told them and then headed back through to the kitchen. He glanced at the farmers in the front of the tea shop. They were still there, as were most of the other customers, all making a night of it having dinner and enjoying the warmth of the fire and the cheery atmosphere.

The farmer interested in Kity had said no more to her, so it seemed as if the situation was fine, but Gordon still kept an eye on him.

Gordon checked the time. Almost nine o'clock. The bee night was nearly finished and Lochlan would be coming down to meet Kity. Glancing back at Kity and the other ladies, he was sure that Lochlan's proposal would be news to them. Smiling to himself, he went into the kitchen and started to clear things up for the night. He had notes on the wedding cake for Poppy and planned to chat to her about this.

Kity was such a fast knitter and had made excellent progress with Eila's bolero.

Pearl had quilted lots more coasters and other members had sewn bags for the favours. Overall, it had been a productive evening.

'I'm going to try embroidering the winter cottage pattern,' Kity told Poppy. 'I saw the new video on your website. I've learned so many techniques from watching you demonstrate stitching the patterns. I've nailed the whipped back stitch.'

Poppy was pleased.

One of the other members spoke up. 'I used your videos to learn French knots. Now I like adding them to my embroidery work.'

'Are there any other knots that I should learn?' Kity said to Poppy.

'Colonial knots,' Poppy told her. 'I've a video on those on my website. And bullion knots.'

'I'll look those up,' Kity promised, eager to learn more. She checked the winter cottage pattern. 'What type of thread did you use for the roof?'

'Crewel wool. White. Satin stitch. Then I highlighted it with strands of silver metallic thread to make it glitter a little as if the roof was covered in shimmering snow. And I used running back stitches to create a sparkling effect on the garden in front of the cottage with the silver thread.'

Several of the members checked the pattern they'd been given by Poppy and noted the embroidery tips.

'What weight of white cotton fabric do you prefer for your embroideries like the winter cottage?' Kity said to Poppy.

'A thread count of 180–200 is my preference, especially for the cotton fabric,' Poppy replied. 'Most of my embroideries fit into six or seven inch hoops, and I cut two pieces of fabric for my work. One for the top embroidery and the other as backing fabric to give the work more substance and to help hide any stray threads. I have videos showing what I do.'

'I'll look those up too,' said Kity.

'You should try adding videos of your knitting techniques to your website,' Poppy suggested.

Kity sighed. 'I've thought about it, but I've been so busy since setting up the shop.'

'I'm sure your customers would enjoy seeing you demonstrate your knitting,' said Poppy.

'I'd watch those,' Eila chipped–in.

'So would I,' said Pearl. 'I love watching sewing and knitting techniques. I find it quite relaxing.'

'Okay, I'll do it,' Kity said firmly. 'I've sometimes thought I'd like to film my knitting in my wee shed, have it set up so I could demonstrate when I had any spare time.'

'That sounds cosy.' Judy pictured Kity ensconced in it knitting away.

'I think with all this snow I'll need a heater for the shed,' said Kity.

'I'm sure Lochlan could sort that out for you,' Minnie told her.

'Yes, I'll mention it to him. And tell him I'm going to make knitting videos.' Kity smiled. 'It could be fun or chaos.'

'A bit of both sounds entertaining,' said Poppy.

Minnie lowered her voice. 'That's Gordon peeking through. A subtle hint that we need to call it a night.'

The ladies packed up their crafts, tidied the function room as usual, leaving nothing for Gordon to clean up. They'd even piled their empty hot chocolate cups on to the trolley and Poppy wheeled it through to the kitchen taking her wedding folder with her.

'I have to talk to Gordon about the wedding cake,' said Poppy as the other ladies put their coats and jackets on ready to brave the cold night.

The members settled their bill with Gordon at the front counter and started to head out.

Kity, Eila and Poppy were the only members left, although customers were still sitting in the tea shop, including the farmers.

Kity and Eila stood within the function room out of their way, chatting about knitting and sewing.

'I should have your bolero knitted in a couple of days,' said Kity.

'Pop into my dress shop when you've time for a fitting. I'd like to get your bridesmaid dress finished.'

'I'll do that. I promise.'

Kity and Eila continued to chat about the dresses for the wedding while Kity waited for Lochlan to arrive. He wasn't late and was due within the next few minutes.

CHAPTER SIX

Lochlan walked across the snow–covered field, a tall, dark figure silhouetted by the glow of the house as he headed down to the shore to meet Kity at the tea shop. Lights shone from the windows of the two–storey building and the traditional architecture was evident even from a distance. The house faced the sea and he'd added a balcony to the upstairs master bedroom. He pictured sitting outside on the balcony on balmy nights gazing out at the sea and enjoying the lingering twilights. With Kity.

A small upstairs lounge offered the same benefits.

Creating the house had been a labour of love in more ways than one. It was hard work without hardship. He'd always been passionate about building and architecture work. And about Kity.

The garden was still a work in progress, but he'd trimmed the hedges that created a natural fence around the edges of the property. The branches of the trees in the back garden were pared to the bone, but they'd soon flourish in the spring and provide back–up to shield the rear of the house.

Although the building had been dilapidated when he'd bought it, the foundations were solid. When he'd effectively torn it to the core, the restructuring had been rewarding.

He'd rebuilt many a house for clients. This was the first time he'd built it to his own design for himself. He'd probably tinker with it in time, especially as the seasons changed, adapting it to suit the milder months.

81

He definitely wanted to build a summerhouse in the garden. He'd seen how much Kity liked her little shed. A summerhouse where they could both relax and enjoy the flowers he planned to have in the garden would be a nice niche.

The kitchen was tucked at the rear of the house and opened out on to the back garden. It was large, square and sturdy, kitted out with plenty of cupboards and storage from the vintage–style dresser to glass–fronted cabinets filled with cups, plates and teapots. The table and chairs were at the window so that sitting having a meal or a cuppa in the kitchen would offer a view of the garden and fields beyond.

Now all he had to do was ask Kity to marry him and share this lovely house together.

He'd showered, shaved and put on clean clothes — black jeans and the grey jumper Kity had knitted for him. His favourite jumper. His dark hair was swept back from his handsome features and he wore a classic winter jacket to thwart the cold night air.

It had stopped snowing hours ago and in the crisp stillness his boots crunched through the icy layers that covered the field and stretched out all around the countryside. The snow glittered in the night's glow like thousands of scattered diamonds.

Striding purposefully away from the house, no one would've guessed that his heart was thundering in his chest. His hot breath burst from his lips and filtered into the icy air as he kept telling himself to calm down. He wasn't usually the anxious type. More down to earth than head in the clouds. But tonight...he was on edge. This was it. After all the years of loving and longing for Kity, from as far back as when they were at school, here he was about to ask her to be his wife.

Until recently, if anyone had asked him whether he had a snowball's chance in a hot frying pan of Kity accepting his offer of marriage, he'd have shook his head. Now, it was a different story. One he hoped had a happy ending. Since she'd opened her knitting shop and he'd walked into her life to mend her shelves, he felt like his life, and hers, had finally settled where he'd always dreamed they could be. If only she didn't think of him as the most annoying boy in the world.

He tried to shrug off his trepidation, but it weighed too heavy to be shifted tonight.

Glancing back at the house, it was aglow with lights inside and out, a beacon of hope. He had to hope that she'd say yes.

Everything was set for a romantic dinner. Candles ready to be lit. A log fire. Lamps casting a cosy glow in the rooms, especially the living room where he intended making his proposal.

Forging on towards the lights on the esplanade, he looked up at the clear, dark sky. A winter moon shone a silvery shimmer across the calm sea. Like him, it was deceivingly calm on the surface, but far off in the distance the underlying ripples of an impending storm looked like it was brewing.

In the morning he intended going for a swim in the icy sea. Maybe Kity would see him and be impressed. Impressing Kity was something he'd always tried to do, and he had no plans to do otherwise.

A narrow path leading down from the fields to the shops on the shore had been well trodden. The hard packed snow was the result of numerous people during the day taking this route up to the cottages and farmhouses that dotted the landscape. It sparkled in the lights from the shops and reminded him of the diamond ring he'd stashed safely in the house.

Taking a deep breath, he headed for the tea shop.

He saw a few of the ladies walking home after their night at the bee, chatting. In the clear air their voices carried and he heard them mention Poppy and Euan's wedding. They sounded excited. He wondered what their reaction would be if his plan to marry Kity before Christmas panned out.

Running a nervous hand through his thick, dark hair, he walked towards the front door of the tea shop. Maybe the troublesome farmer would be there. Maybe not. His focus was on walking Kity back to the house and doing something that would change their lives for ever.

He'd confided to Dougal about his plan, and his uncle's reaction had been great, wishing him all the best. Telling Gordon was a risk, but he trusted that he wouldn't say anything to Kity or the ladies to spark their suspicions.

Through the tea shop windows he saw that it was still busy with customers, including a table where a farmer he recognised was seated with others. Perhaps one of them had been the man to make a play for Kity.

He opened the door and walked in, looking for Kity, not looking for trouble.

Lochlan's intense blue eyes lanced the farmers seated at the table. The guilty look on one of their faces highlighted the man who'd decided to challenge him for Kity's affections.

Seeing the tall, lean, strong figure walking past them, they decided they'd enjoyed themselves enough at the tea shop, put their jackets on and headed out.

One problem down.

One more to go. Finding a way to walk Kity to the house without arousing her suspicions that he was up to any secret plans.

And there she was, chatting to Eila.

Kity smiled round at Lochlan, pleased to see him.

She shrugged her craft bag on to her shoulder, buttoned her warm coat up and said goodnight to Eila.

It was usual for Eila to spend time with Gordon after the bee and the tea shop was closed. They'd head upstairs and relax together, maybe watch a film and have a late supper.

Gordon was in the kitchen talking to Poppy about her wedding cake, so Lochlan and Kity left without interrupting them.

Lochlan opened the front door for Kity and they stepped outside, illuminated by the glow of the tea shop lanterns.

'Did you have a nice evening?' he said to her.

'I did. Poppy gave me a lovely pattern to embroider a winter cottage. And we got lots done, even though Gordon plied us with tea, cake and hot chocolate.'

She smiled up at him and it eased the thundering of his heart, for a moment, then he knew he'd have to stick to his plan without wavering.

He checked she had her boots on. 'Are you okay to walk up to the house?'

'Yes, I love snowy nights. And it's stopped snowing. It feels like Christmas.' She sounded excited and it made him smile at her.

They walked away from the tea shop, past the bar restaurant and before reaching the knitting shop they veered up the narrow path leading to the fields.

Kity filled her lungs with the fresh air and glanced back at the sea. 'It looks like shimmering silver.' Then she looked up at the vast, dark, star–sprinkled sky. 'The stars shine so bright here. I feel like I could reach up and touch them.'

'It's a fine night.' One to remember, he thought. 'Let me carry your bag,' he offered.

She let him carry it. 'It's wonderful that you've finished the house. I'm excited to see what you've done with it.' Then she stepped on a rut in the snow. 'Have you sorted the holes? Is it okay to walk across the field and the garden now?'

His heart jolted, wishing he hadn't needed to fib about these things, but it was the only way he knew to keep his plans secret.

'Take my arm. It's safe to walk here now, but the snow is thick in patches so hang on to me so you don't tumble.'

Kity was happy to link her arm through his, and gave him a squeeze, smiling up at him, clearly excited to see the house.

They walked up the pathway for a minute or two and then she reacted when she saw the house away ahead of them.

'It's all lit up!' she exclaimed, seeing it aglow against the vast blanket of snow. The winter moon cast it in a blue–white light, creating a picture perfect scene that was worthy of being on a Christmas card.

She paused. 'You should take a photo of the house like this.'

He nodded and took his phone out and snapped a couple of pictures. He checked the images and she peered at them too.

'The pictures are lovely,' she commented.

'Yes, but there's something missing.'

Kity frowned. 'What?'

'You.'

She smiled at him.

'Stand there with the house in the background so I can include you in the pictures,' he said.

Kity posed happily, even scooping up a handful of snow and making it into a snowball, pretending to throw it.

He clicked the shot, capturing Kity, the real Kity he knew and loved. Full of mischief and beauty.

'Let me take pictures of you too,' she insisted, dropping the snowball.

Relieving him of his phone, and taking charge of her bag again, she clicked several shots of Lochlan standing in the snow, looking the most handsome she'd probably ever seen him.

'Now take one of us together.' She gave him his phone back and snuggled close to him, smiling cheerily.

These were the pictures he liked the most. The two of them together with the house in the background.

The night sky was sprinkled with hundreds of stars. It was one of the things Kity loved about living in the Scottish Highlands — seeing the starry skies.

Every evening, unless it was overcast by a storm, she would look out her windows at the stars twinkling in the clear night sky. The autumn months had their own beauty, but in winter there was a crispness to the air that added clarity to the stars.

Trudging on, the snow became deeper the closer they came to the house.

Kity slowed down, being careful where she walked, still wary of those holes he'd warned her about.

Scooping her up into his strong arms, he walked the rest of the way, carrying her across the snow.

Kity giggled and had no objection. She put her arms round his shoulders and relished the fun of it.

'The lights around the porch are gorgeous,' she said as he walked up to the front entrance with her still in his arms. 'And I like the vintage lantern.'

He was happy she approved.

'It'll look even better once I put the Christmas lights and decorations up, but it's a little early for that. Maybe next week.'

'I'll help if you want. I enjoy putting up decorations.'

He nodded, put her down gently and dug out his key to open the front door.

Kity stepped inside, admiring the decor and lighting, so warm and welcoming.

'It's a beautiful house, Lochlan.' She gazed around in awe. 'I love the colour scheme, the decor and the furniture.'

He smiled at her. 'So you approve of what I've done?'

'With bells on,' she chirped, wandering through to the lounge. 'Oh, I should've taken my boots off. I don't want to spoil your lovely floor and rugs.'

'It's okay,' he assured her.

Kity stepped out of her boots and padded around in her socks.

'Let me take your jacket.' He hung her jacket up along with his.

'I see you're still getting a lot of wear out of that jumper. I need to knit you another one. Would you like a classic, Shetland wool jumper for Christmas?'

'Yes, I'd love anything you'd knit for me.'

'Don't tempt me to be a rascal and knit you a gaudy Christmas jumper,' she teased him.

'I'd still wear it.'

'You would, wouldn't you.'

'If you knitted it, yes.'

Her smiled lit up his heart.

Come on, he urged himself. Guide her over to the fire and light the candles for dinner.

'Candles! How romantic.' She seemed happy, but thought it was to celebrate that he'd completed the house.

'Something smells tasty,' she said. The aroma from the dinner he'd prepared earlier wafted through from the kitchen. It was ready to reheat and serve.

'I thought we could have dinner.'

She frowned, seeing the look in his eyes, as if dinner wasn't his priority right now.

'Is everything okay, Lochlan?'

He took her hands in his and gazed down at her. 'There's something I'd like to talk to you about.'

She blinked up at him with interest, unaware that he was poised to propose.

'Yes?' she said.

'I'd like to ask you...' He found his voice stalling, wondering if he should tell her how much he loved her first and then pop the question. Or the other way around. He'd planned it all in his head, but in real life, his emotions cast his senses to the wind and he decided to come right out with it and tell her how he felt about her.

'You know I love you, Kity,' he began.

She did. 'I love you too.'

His heart notched into the hopeful zone.

Okay, here goes...

He lifted the ring box where he'd left it and got down on one knee in front of the log fire.

Kity's green eyes reflected the light from the fire as she realised what he was doing.

Opening the box so that she could see the scintillating diamond ring, he took a steadying breath. 'Kity, will you marry me?'

She thought her heart would burst with happiness. 'Yes! I'd love to marry you.'

Everything he hoped for and everything he'd dreamed of came true in that moment.

He placed the ring on her finger. It fitted. He'd gone to a lot of trouble trying to find out what her ring size was, and had got it right.

'It's a beautiful ring.' She held her hand out and watched it sparkle in the warmth of the candlelight and lamps.

He kissed her and wrapped her in his arms.

Now he just had to reveal the other part of his plan.

'I'm pleased you like the ring, Kity. But there's one more thing I need to ask you.'

She couldn't figure out what that could be. 'Okay.'

'You love the winter. I know you'd like to be a Christmas bride, a December bride, whatever you want to call it.'

'So you're thinking we could get married next year at Christmas?' She loved that idea.

'No...*this Christmas*.'

She blinked, thinking she'd misheard or misunderstood. 'But Christmas is only a few weeks away.'

'I've got the paperwork information and if we start to notify our intention to get married, we could plan our wedding for three days after Poppy and Euan's marriage.' He had all sorts of explanations what they needed and why they should do it. They could get married in the new house. A small but romantic ceremony. Invite close friends and his uncle. Organise a party as their reception. Have a Christmas honeymoon at home and head off on holiday in the New Year if she wanted. He reeled them off.

'Okay,' she cut–in and smiled excitedly.

'You'll do it?' He needed to confirm that he'd heard right.

She nodded firmly. 'Yes.'

'Everyone will think we're impulsive, that we should wait—'

'But it's our wedding, our decision.'

Lochlan lifted her up and swung her around as if she was light as a feather and then put her down gently. 'I'm so happy.'

Kity stepped close to him and put her arms around his shoulders. On tip toes she reached up and kissed him. 'So am I.'

He led her over to the dinner table, popped open a bottle of champagne, poured two glasses and handed one to her.

They tipped their glasses in a celebratory toast and she giggled as bubbles tickled her nose when she sipped her drink.

He was about to head through to the kitchen to sort the dinner, and then paused. 'Would you mind if I messaged Dougal to tell him the good news? He knows I was going to ask you this evening.'

'Tell him, let him know,' she insisted.

Lochlan messaged Dougal and then went into the kitchen to start heating and serving up the dinner he'd prepared.

Kity followed him through.

'Can I give you a hand?' she offered.

'No, you sit down and enjoy your champagne.'

She sat down at the kitchen table and watched him heat the casserole in the oven.

'It's nothing too fancy,' he said. 'Just a casserole and potatoes. I know you've been at the tea shop having tea and cakes—'

'I did more knitting and chatting than munching cakes, though I did indulge a little. But this smells delicious.' And she loved that he'd made the effort to prepare dinner for them.

He cast a loving smile over to her, melting her heart.

She admired her ring and sipped her drink. 'I really love this ring. Does anyone else know, apart from Dougal, that you were planning to propose tonight?'

'I told Gordon. He phoned to tip me off that the farmer was chatting you up, and I confided in him. He said he'd keep my secret.'

'He did. I'd no idea what you were planning.' Then she thought about Gordon. 'Do you want to tell him I said yes? He's bound to be wondering.'

Lochlan took out his phone. 'I'll let him know.' He typed the message. *Kity said yes!* He pressed send and then put his phone in his pocket.

They were chatting when a few minutes later Gordon replied. *Congratulations to you and Kity! Is it still a secret?*

'Gordon wants to know if our news is a secret,' Lochlan told Kity.

She shook her head. 'Everyone is going to find out when they see this sparkler on my finger tomorrow.'

No, it's not a secret, Lochlan clarified, and then began serving up their dinner.

They sat at the dining table in the living room having dinner by candlelight and Lochlan topped up their glasses with champagne.

Gordon smiled as he clicked his phone off.

'You seem happy,' Eila said to him as they snuggled on the sofa watching a film. 'What is it?'

'Lochlan has asked Kity to marry him, and she's accepted.'

Eila's face broke into a delighted smile. 'That's wonderful! They're a lovely couple.'

'He proposed to her at his new house tonight. He told me when I phoned him earlier this evening, but I promised not to tell. I asked him if it's still a secret but he says no it's not.'

Eila took out her phone. 'I'm messaging Kity to congratulate her.'

Eila's message popped up on Kity's phone. She glanced at it and smiled. 'Eila has sent her congratulations. Gordon must've told her.' She read a second message from Eila. 'She wants to know what the ring is like.'

'Tell her.' He could see that Kity was eager to let her friend know about her ring.

Kity snapped a quick picture of her ring and sent it to Eila.

It's gorgeous! Eila replied.

Kity relayed Eila's reaction.

Lochlan tucked into his dinner and smiled, pleased that he'd chosen the right type of ring for Kity.

As they ate their dinner, messages started to light up both their phones, causing them to laugh as the gossip caught fire throughout the village.

'It'll save us having to make an announcement in the morning,' said Kity. 'The whirlwind will be wild enough when the ladies at the bee, and others, find out we're getting married.'

Lochlan gave her a mischievous smile. 'Wait until they know that we've set a date for a week before Christmas.'

Kity blinked, thinking he was right, and then she laughed. 'This is going to be fun.'

Lochlan topped up their glasses again. 'My ears are burning already.'

Minnie was sitting beside the fire in her cottage drinking a mug of cocoa when her phone rang.

She checked the time and frowned, wondering who was calling at this time of night. It was Pearl.

Minnie clutched at her dressing gown. 'Pearl? What's wrong? Has something happened?'

'Nothing. And yes,' Pearl replied. 'Judy's just phoned to tell me the news—Kity and Lochlan are engaged.'

'Engaged? Are you sure?' Minnie was pleased but thought that this type of gossip would've filtered through her shop before others found out.

'I'm sending you a picture that Eila sent to Poppy, and then Poppy sent to Judy, and Judy sent it a few minutes ago to me.' Pearl sounded breathless with excitement.

Minnie looked at the picture of the engagement ring and gasped. 'What a dazzler!'

Bracken was snuggled up in his basket, but his ears pricked hearing Minnie's astonishment.

'It's okay, Bracken.' Minnie patted his head to reassure him.

'It's a beautiful ring,' Pearl agreed. 'Lochlan proposed to Kity at his house this evening. She thought she was going there to see the house all finished, but he'd set it up for a romantic proposal. We don't have the details.'

'We'll glean those tomorrow. But I'm going to message Kity now.'

Ending their call, Minnie sent a message to Kity. *Congratulations on your engagement! Your ring is beautiful.*

Kity read Minnie's message. 'Minnie sends her congratulations and she loves the ring too.'

'Word travels really fast around here.' Lochlan grinned and relaxed back in his chair.

Poppy phoned Euan at his farmhouse. 'I've just heard the news that Lochlan asked Kity to marry him and she said yes.'

'That's great. I think they'll be a happy couple.'

'So that will be another local wedding to look forward to,' Poppy told him. 'Pearl was saying this evening at the bee that it would be nice to have another wedding to make things for. Looks like she got her wish.'

Euan sent Lochlan his congratulations.

The messages from well–wishers continued to light up Lochlan and Kity's phones, and they enjoyed these special moments.

'Jock sends us his best,' Lochlan told Kity. 'He wants to talk to me in the morning.'

'About what?' Kity was curious.

Lochlan shrugged. 'I'll pop in to see him after I've gone for a morning swim.'

Kity balked. 'You're really going to swim in the snow cold sea?'

Lochlan cast her a sexy smile. 'I want to impress my fianceé.'

She gestured around her, to the meal, the house, the ring. 'I'm impressed enough.'

'Nah! I'm braving the sea to celebrate.'

She knew that cheeky grin of his, and steeled herself not to shiver or flinch when she saw him swimming in the morning. And to be extremely impressed with her husband–to–be. Even the thought of these words sent a ripple of excitement through her.

Lochlan stood up from the table and pulled her close for a loving embrace. 'I'm so impressed with you, Kity. Saying yes to marrying me at Christmastime.'

'Do you think we should tell everyone that news?' Kity said to him, sounding as if she thought they should.

Lochlan took a deep breath. 'I'll message Gordon.' He lit the touch paper as he sent the message telling Gordon they were getting married — this Christmas.

Gordon jolted as he read the message. 'Lochlan says they're getting married at Christmas,' he told Eila.

'Next Christmas,' Eila said sleepily. It was getting late and she was snuggled up cosy on the sofa with Gordon, resting her head on his shoulder. 'Another Christmas bride. That will be lovely.'

Gordon shook his head. 'No,' he emphasised. 'This Christmas!'

CHAPTER SEVEN

Judy sounded aghast as she took the call from Minnie. Jock was tending to customers at the bar, but the premises was due to close soon.

'Married before Christmas!' Judy's voice initiated a few curious glances from customers in the bar. She called over to Jock above the sound of the music playing in the background. 'Kity and Lochlan are getting married a week before Christmas.'

Jock almost spilled the pint of beer he was pouring. 'Are you sure?'

'Yes,' Judy insisted, walking closer to him. 'It's not gossip. Lochlan told Gordon. He told Eila, and then the news spread through the bee members. Minnie assures me it's true.'

Minnie was still on the phone. 'We'll find out all the details of the proposal tomorrow.'

'What about a wedding dress for Kity, their reception, the flowers...' Judy reeled off several things that would need to be done.

'Lochlan seems to have planned it,' Minnie explained. 'And Kity is delighted to be a Christmas bride. I don't know about a wedding dress or anything else. I would suppose that Kity could buy a dress from a bridal shop in one of the towns.'

'When I spoke to Kity earlier today I asked her what type of wedding dress she'd like. She said her perfect dress would be white chiffon. But she'd no idea that Lochlan was going to propose tonight.'

'Do you think they'll have a big, fancy reception?' said Minnie.

'No, Kity said she'd like a small, intimate wedding. She told me she'd be happy with a beautiful dress, a wedding cake and the man of her dreams.'

'Well, she's got Lochlan, so now all she needs is the dress and the cake.' Minnie sighed. 'It's getting late. I'm up early so I'll talk to you about this in the morning.'

'Okay, we'll speak then.'

After the call, Judy helped Jock at the bar, pouring the final glasses of whisky of the night, but her mind was whirring with the news.

'I can hear your brain burling,' Jock said to her, leaning close. 'Is it about the wedding?'

'Yes, I'd like to pop upstairs to check on something.'

'I'll finish up the orders.'

'Are you sure?' The bar was fairly busy.

'Aye, on ye go,' Jock urged her.

Leaving Jock to tend to the bar, Judy went upstairs, flicked the lights on and lifted up her wedding dress sketch book. She opened it at the dress that Kity had said was so classy. A traditional style with a soft flowing skirt.

Looking at it with a dressmaker's eye, she pictured she could make it in white chiffon. It wouldn't take her long to make such a classic style of dress. In comparison to Poppy's fabulous satin dress with the invisible neckline, sleeves and fitted bodice encrusted with sparkle, the traditional chiffon bridal gown would be far easier to make. She'd made evening dresses that were similar in structure.

Pulling down a folder full of all the paper patterns for dresses she'd made, she rummaged through it and found one that she could easily adapt.

Judy scribbled notes, estimating the amount of fabric needed. Years of dressmaking experience came into play, and by the time Jock came trudging up the stairs to see if she'd got lost in one of her wardrobes, she had a plan for Kity's dress.

'Ah, there you are,' Jock announced, grinning at her. 'I thought I'd have to fight my way through your wardrobes in search of you.'

'Sorry, I got lost in my designs.' She showed him the sketch of the lovely wedding dress and the paper pattern.

'For Kity, I presume.'

'If she wants it. I could make it without too much fuss in time for her wedding. It's a fairly classic design. The beauty is in the dreamlike quality of the layers of chiffon on the skirt.'

'It's a beauty,' he agreed. 'Very different from Poppy's dress from what you've told me.'

'Yes, and Eila has rolls of white chiffon fabric in her dress shop, so I wouldn't even need to order the fabric. It's right there in Eila's shop.'

'Kity's a lovely lass. If she wants the dress and you can make it, do it. We'll give it to her as a wedding gift.'

Judy put her sketch book aside, stood up and put her arms around Jock's shoulders. 'That's a great idea.' She smiled and gave him a kiss.

'Right, let's lock up for the night and get home for some rest. I've a feeling tomorrow is going to be hectic.'

Flicking the lights off, Judy followed Jock downstairs and they headed home together, chatting about the two weddings.

Poppy phoned Euan at his farmhouse again. 'I've just heard from Minnie that Kity and Lochlan are getting married a week before Christmas.'

'That's fast.'

'I know, but I think it's exciting. And I feel that all the focus will be shared between the two weddings now, and that sort of takes the pressure off of us.'

Euan thought about this for a moment and then agreed. 'That's right. I'm certainly happy that we're not the only ones getting married at Christmastime.'

'I'm glad you feel the same as me.'

'Do you have any details of what they're planning for the reception?'

'No, but it'll be the topic of local gossip in the morning for sure. I'm quite keen to find out what their wedding plans are.'

Euan looked out the window of his study where he'd been working late. 'I thought there was going to be a storm tonight but it's blown by us. But make sure to keep the cottage warm. There's probably going to be more snow overnight.'

'I'll do that. Oh, and I spoke to Gordon about our wedding cake. He showed me his sketches. His ideas are wonderful. One in particular is lovely. A traditional design, three–tier cake. The bottom layer would be fruit cake, and the other two tiers vanilla sponge with strawberry jam and buttercream. And white icing with pink and white fondant roses.'

'It sounds ideal.'

'I'll show you the sketches tomorrow.'

After their call, Poppy sat by the fire pouring over her wedding folder. She never thought she'd find so much enjoyment planning the wedding. All the little details were in the folder and she aimed to keep it long after they were married. A treasured keepsake.

Sighing, she forced herself to close the folder and went to bed.

Gazing out the bedroom window she saw snowflakes falling outside and snuggled under the covers. Euan was right. It was going to snow overnight.

Lochlan walked Kity home to the knitting shop. All the shops and the bar restaurant were closed for the night.

Far in the distance the storm seemed to have rained down further along the coast, avoiding the village.

'I think the thunder storm has moved past us,' said Lochlan. 'But it's starting to snow.'

Kity had her arm linked through his and snuggled into him. 'I'm happy with more snow.'

The shoulders of his jacket were sprinkled with flakes by the time they headed into the knitting shop. He went through to the back of the shop and stood there so as not to get any snow on the lovely yarn.

'I'll get those documents you need for our marriage application.' Kity ran upstairs to get them, leaving Lochlan to look out the back window at her shed. He had a spare lantern that he could fit beside the front door.

Lochlan was still planning things for the shed when she came back down with the documents.

He put them in his jacket pocket. 'I'll get all the paperwork posted away tomorrow. Start the ball rolling.' Then he mentioned his plans for the shed.

'I think I'll need a heater,' she told him.

'There's a heater in the shed.'

'Where?' She hadn't seen it.

'I saw it a wee while ago, the last time I was in there putting a light inside the shed for you. It's up on the top shelf.'

Despite it being late, snowing, and that she was still buzzing from the proposal, she wanted to see where the heater was.

They went out to the shed, turned the light on and he lifted it down. A small heater, but just what she needed.

He plugged it into the power connection he'd installed for the lighting, and within moments it started to glow with warmth.

'It'll need to burn off some of the dust from not being used in a while, but then it'll be nice and cosy in the shed.' He angled it so that the heat would circulate around and be near enough her chair to keep her snug.

'This is great. I didn't know it was there.' She reached out her cold hands and felt the warmth.

Lochlan looked around. 'You've got this well organised. It's a great wee nook for your knitting.'

'I love it.'

He told her about his plans for a summerhouse.

Kity's eyes showed her delight. 'A shed at the shop and a summerhouse at home.'

Lochlan's heart reacted hearing her refer to the house he'd build as home.

'Would you like a cup of tea before you go?' Kity offered him.

'No, it's getting really late. We should both get some sleep.'

Kity turned the heater and the light off in the shed and they went inside and through to the front of the shop.

Lochlan kissed her and got ready to leave. 'It's been the best night of my life, Kity.'

Her engagement ring sparkled in the light and she kept feeling the urge to admire it. 'I keep looking at my ring. I can't quite believe we're engaged. It's like a winter fairytale.'

'A fairytale come true.' He pulled her into his arms and held her tight.

They kissed goodnight, and he went to leave, but Kity said, 'Are you really planning to go swimming in the sea in the morning?'

'Yes, I want to impress you,' he joked.

'You impressed me tonight,' she said lovingly. 'You created a lasting impression. I'll never forget this evening.'

They kissed again, and he headed out into the snow, waving, and walking back up to the house.

Kity switched the shop lights off and went upstairs.

In her little kitchen, she made herself a cup of tea. She was too excited to sleep.

Sitting on the sofa by the fire, she knitted a few more rows of the bolero and thought about everything that had happened that night. Lochlan's romantic proposal rewound in her mind. And for the first time ever, she felt what it was like to knit while wearing a beautiful diamond engagement ring.

Smiling to herself, she knitted late into the night, enjoying the warmth of the fire and thinking about getting married.

She thought about what she'd said to Judy about a chiffon wedding dress, a wedding cake and the man of her dreams. Little did she know what Lochlan was planning. Now they had to plan for their big day. A small version. She imagined that they'd order a cake from the tea shop. Gordon's cakes were marvellous.

With two things tick boxed — the man of her dreams and the wedding cake, all she needed was the dress.

Putting her knitting aside, she opened her laptop and began scrolling through dresses in bridal shops. The selections were lovely, but...

No, she scolded herself. She couldn't possibly ask Judy to make that dress design in the sketch book. It was perfect though...and chiffon was her dream fabric...

But Judy was still working on finishing Poppy's dress, so she pushed her thoughts of this aside and continued to scroll through the dresses before finally heading to bed.

Unsure whether to wear her ring in bed or not, she decided to err on the side of caution and put it safely in the little ring box that Lochlan had given her — and watched the snow falling outside the window to calm her excitement so she could fall asleep.

Gordon couldn't sleep, too restless to settle, thinking over his relationship with Eila. He wanted to pick up the phone and talk to her, but she'd gone home to her dress shop and would be sound asleep by now.

Throwing the quilt back he got up and padded through to the kitchen to make himself a mug of warm milk. The bee ladies had made the patchwork for him and he appreciated the work they'd put into it.

He wore the bottom half of his pyjamas and a pale blue semmit. The vest showed the well–worked muscles in his chest, shoulders and arms. Hard work running the tea shop was responsible for most of his lean musculature, with the remainder accrued from this early morning swims. Swimming was invigorating. His daily dips set him up for the day. Sometimes he wished he could go night swimming, but the tea shop opening hours prevented fitting this into his schedule.

Standing at the front window in the glow shining through from the kitchen to the living room, he drank his milk and pondered the possibility of going for a swim right there and then.

Snow or no snow, he was sorely tempted, but sensibility prevailed and he stayed where he was drinking his milk and wondering if he was doing the right thing regarding Eila. In truth, he'd happily marry her tomorrow.

He gazed out at the snow drifting over the sea. A spring or summer wedding sounded lovely, something special to plan for and look forward to. But now with Kity and Lochlan tying the knot at Christmastime too, and a New Year wedding in the works for Abby and Josh...it made him ponder...should Eila and him dive right in and get married in December?

He downed the remainder of his milk and shook the thoughts from his mind.

Putting his unsettledness down to the whirlwind news of another local wedding, he went back to bed and forced himself to be tired.

Lochlan lingered in the shower, letting the warm water wash away the strains of the day. Feeling the tense muscles in his strong shoulders and back uncoil, he realised how wound up he'd been from getting the house ready to propose to Kity.

He looked up, eyes closed, and let it wash over his face then got ready to finish as always with a cold shower. One or two minutes blast of cold water over his whole body, he believed, helped keep him strong and capable of tackling the elements when he was working outdoors. Scottish winters could be challenging, but he'd made himself hardy, and he actually enjoyed the cold showers, feeling energised after stepping out.

The en suite bathroom off the master bedroom had a walk–in shower for two, plus a scalloped corner bath with overhead shower.

He shook the water from his silky dark hair, stepped into flip flops, and threw on a towelling robe.

The view from the bedroom showed the snowy seascape, reminding him that he was swimming in the

108

morning. Picking up his phone, he sent Gordon a message.

I'm going swimming in the morning. You up for it?

He didn't expect such a speedy reply, but Gordon hadn't managed to fall asleep yet.

Count me in. Snow swimming by the looks of it.

All the better to impress Kity.

And Eila.

See you at the crack of dawn, Gordon.

It'll be baltic. Gordon's warning didn't deter Lochlan.

Oh, yes.

Despite having a late night, Kity was up extra early and busy in the knitting shop. Two reasons.

One — wedding excitement, knowing Minnie, Judy and others would be wanting to hear all about Lochlan's proposal. She was well up for telling them all the details, and showing them her beautiful ring that was now on her hand again.

Two — if Lochlan was going swimming, she didn't want to miss it.

No sooner had the latter thought skimmed through her mind than she looked out the front window and saw Lochlan striding down to the shore wearing charcoal joggers, training shoes and not much else. A rolled up towel was tucked under his arm and a small rucksack was his only accessory.

Her heart fluttered seeing him. He was such a fine looking man. Foolhardy at times, like this morning, but a heartbreaker for sure.

109

As if sensing her watching him, he suddenly looked round. Seeing her peer through the window of her knitting shop, he waved to her.

Kity waved back, shivering at the thought of what he was about to do.

Snow falling overnight had added another layer of sparkling white to everything. And it was still snowing gently. Flakes were whipped away in the icy breeze.

Then she saw Gordon join him, similarly dressed.

They stood chatting for a moment, nodded firmly and then they both stripped down to their trunks, kicked their shoes off and walked towards the icy sea.

Kity watched them stride into the water in tandem, each backing the other up, and then they dived into it, submerging for a few moments before bobbing to the surface, laughing.

Lochlan waved again at Kity and she acknowledged she'd seen him dip below the cold surface. A light grey sky draped itself over the landscape and a pale sun tried and failed to make itself a shining example of warmth.

She noticed Gordon waving to someone too and realised that Eila was watching him from the window of her dress shop.

Snowflakes blew by the window of the knitting shop and Kity shivered just thinking about how cold the sea was bound to be.

Lochlan called over to Gordon as they swam around. 'It's warmer under the surface. I feel the icy blast whenever I stand up.'

'I know. It's deceiving. The hardest bit will be when we have to walk back up to the esplanade.'

They swam a fair distance along the shoreline, and then turned and headed back.

Striding out of the sea, they both tried not to shiver as they walked back to where they'd left their towels and clothes. They used the shower stands to wash off the salt water.

Gordon's teeth were chattering as he dried himself roughly at speed.

Lochlan set a personal record for drying off and getting dressed.

They both waved to Kity and Eila.

'Cheers for joining me this morning,' Lochlan said to Gordon.

'I'm firing up the skillet for fresh pancakes and eggs. Once you've strutted your stuff at Kity's shop, drop by for a warm breakfast.'

'I'll do that,' Lochlan said eagerly.

CHAPTER EIGHT

Lochlan headed over to Kity's shop, smiling as he saw that she was watching him through the front window.

He stepped inside and stood near the door looking fit and energised. 'I won't come near your yarn.' He swept his hand through his damp hair pushing it back from his face, and dug out a fleece jacket from his rucksack and shrugged it on.

'That was impressive,' she said, smiling at him. 'I'm still shivering from watching you and Gordon.'

He noticed she was wearing her engagement ring.

She held it up and exaggerated how it sparkled under the lights. 'I've had messages from Minnie and Judy saying they want to see the ring this morning.'

'I'm going to post the documents at the post office when it opens.' He patted the rucksack where he'd stashed the envelope safely.

'Would you like a cup of tea to heat you up?' she offered. 'I was going to put the kettle on before I start work.'

He thumbed behind him. 'Gordon's offered me a cooked breakfast. But do you want to come with me? I'm sure he'd be happy for you to join us.'

'No, I've had a bowl of porridge and need to get the day started so that I can dart back and forth to see Minnie and the others while getting some work done.'

Lochlan zipped up his fleece, shrugged on his rucksack and leaned down carefully to kiss her without soaking her with his damp hair.

'I'll see you later and we'll start making plans for the wedding,' he said. 'Do you want me to ask Gordon if he'd make us a cake?'

'Yes. Any idea what type you'd like?'

'No, all wedding cakes look nice to me. What would you prefer?'

'At such short notice I don't want to put Gordon to any bother. I'd be happy with a two–tier vanilla sponge cake with white icing.'

'I'll tell Gordon.'

Kity smiled. 'I'm going to indulge in buying bridal magazines from Minnie's shop if she has any left.'

He loved hearing the excitement in her voice.

'So be prepared to be deluged with bridal features galore.'

He laughed, kissed her again and headed out.

The snow swirled around him as he walked to the tea shop. It wasn't open to customers yet, but he went in and followed the tasty aroma of cooking wafting from the kitchen.

'Great timing. The pancakes and eggs are ready.' Gordon had set up two plates at the kitchen table.

Lochlan put his rucksack out the way and sat down, enjoying the warmth of the kitchen. 'Thanks for this, Gordon.'

Pouring mugs of tea, Gordon served up two plates of pancakes, eggs and cooked tomatoes along with bread and butter. 'Tuck in.'

Lochlan did. 'I've worked up quite an appetite.'

Gordon joined him. 'I wasn't planning to go snow swimming, but I'm feeling fit from it, and hungry.' He

113

started to eat his breakfast. 'Eila was watching us,' he mumbled. 'She says she was impressed.'

'So was Kity. And she said to ask you if you'd make us a wedding cake. Nothing too fancy. We don't want to cause you a load of work.'

Gordon waved his fork as if making them a cake wasn't a bother. 'I love making wedding and birthday cakes. What type did you have in mind?'

Lochlan rattled off Kity's idea. 'A two–tier vanilla sponge cake with white icing.'

'I can make that. Nae bother.'

Lochlan scooped scrambled eggs on to a slice of thick–cut buttered bread. 'I appreciate it. That's one thing organised.'

'Are you having a reception after the wedding ceremony?'

Lochlan drank down a mouthful of tea. 'Nothing's planned. We talked last night after I proposed. We sort of thought we'd have a small but romantic ceremony at the new house. We'd invite close friends and Dougal. I suppose we'd organise a party there as our reception.'

'That could work,' Gordon agreed, but he had another idea. 'If it's only for a few guests, say around twenty or so, you could have your reception here at the tea shop.'

Lochlan's eyes lit up. 'You'd do that?'

'Yes, I've had various private events in the tea shop. If you got married let's say in the early afternoon at your house, you could all come down to the tea shop in the late afternoon. I'd close the premises in the afternoon.'

'That sounds ideal. It's a yes from me.'

'Talk it over with Kity and let me know.'

'I will.' Lochlan tucked into his breakfast feeling as if the wedding plans were forging ahead.

Gordon fell quiet and Lochlan sensed something was wrong.

'Are you okay, Gordon?'

'Yes,' he said unconvincingly and then confided. 'I couldn't settle down to sleep last night. I kept wondering if I should encourage Eila to get married now rather than wait until the spring or the summer.'

'Is this because we're getting married as well as Poppy and Euan?'

Gordon didn't lie. 'Yes. Seeing other couples getting wed made me realise how much I'd love to marry Eila now. But I don't want to rush her into it. I think she wants to look forward to all the planning.'

'Have you spoken to her about this?'

'I wanted to phone her last night, but it was really late and I didn't want to wake her up.'

'You should talk to her,' Lochlan advised.

Gordon nodded and cupped his mug of tea. 'She ran in here earlier to say she'd been watching me swimming from the window of her dress shop. She was so chirpy. I didn't like to bring up any heavy topics.'

'Talk to her later, but if you want my opinion, if Eila wants to enjoy all the wedding planning, you'd maybe be better waiting until the spring. But there's nothing to stop you planning wee things now. Kity's buying bridal magazines from Minnie's shop. Perhaps you should buy a copy for Eila, let her get started well in advance for her wedding.'

Gordon's attitude brightened. 'That's the perfect suggestion. Does Minnie's grocery shop sell many bridal magazines?'

'I've no idea.'

'I'll pop along and have a peek. Surprise Eila with a copy.'

Lochlan smiled and then wondered if he should do the same.

'Are you thinking what I'm thinking?' said Gordon, clearing their plates away.

Lochlan nodded and checked the time. The grocery shop would be open now. 'Shall we?'

Heading out into the cold, they hurried along to Minnie's shop.

She looked startled seeing the pair of them bursting in.

Bracken perked up, ready for attention from them.

Lochlan patted Bracken's head while Gordon scanned the magazine rack.

'What are you two up to?' said Minnie.

'Bridal magazines,' Gordon summarised. 'Do you have any?'

'Yes, I've three copies of that one next to the fashion magazine, and a couple of copies of another bridal publication.'

Gordon grabbed two copies of one and two of the other. He put a set each on the counter.

Lochlan stood up from fussing with Bracken and lifted his copies.

'What's going on?' Minnie said as she rang Gordon's purchase through the till and then charged the other two to Lochlan.

'These are for Kity,' Lochlan explained.

'I gathered that. She's coming in to let me see her ring.' She glanced at Gordon.

'I thought Eila would like to start planning for our wedding,' Gordon told her.

Minnie smiled knowingly to herself. 'Do the pair of you want me to order in any other bridal magazines? The latest issues when they come out.'

'Yes, thanks Minnie,' said Gordon.

'The same goes for me,' Lochlan added.

Minnie noted this down in her order book. 'Done. They should be here in a couple of days.'

Smiling and happy with their purchases, Gordon patted Bracken on the way out.

'The post office is open,' said Lochlan. 'I've something to post, so I'll see you later when I've talked to Kity about having our reception at the tea shop.'

Shivering in the cold as he was only wearing his white shirt and black trousers, Gordon nodded and walked away clutching the magazines.

Hurrying past the tea shop, Gordon continued on to Eila's dress shop. It was locked and he knocked on the window.

Eila came through from the back of the premises where she lived and smiled when she saw Gordon.

She unlocked the door and welcomed him in.

'I thought you might like these.' Gordon thrust the magazines at her.

Eila eyes lit up with interest and she smiled at him. 'I've held back from buying bridal magazines as I didn't want you to think that I was pushing you to set a date.'

'Well, you've mentioned that you'd be happy with a spring or summer wedding.' He gestured to the magazines. 'But I thought it would be nice to begin planning, maybe get some ideas from these.'

Eila started to look through the contents of the magazines.

'I have to get back to the tea shop, but I wanted you to have these now.'

Eila gave him a kiss and an appreciative hug. 'Thanks for these, Gordon.'

Hurrying back to the tea shop, Gordon smiled to himself. Swimming when it was snowing. A potential wedding reception to plan for the tea shop. A two–tier wedding cake to make. And magazines for Eila. He'd done not bad considering it was so early that his tea shop wasn't open yet to customers.

Lochlan handed the bridal magazines to Kity as he walked into the knitting shop after he'd been to the post office. 'I got these for you at Minnie's shop.'

Kity smiled. 'Thank you.' She couldn't wait to pour through them.

'Gordon says he'll make the two–tier wedding cake,' Lochlan confirmed. 'And he says he'd be happy for us to have our reception in the tea shop.' He explained the details.

'Tell Gordon yes please,' Kity confirmed.

'I will.' He checked the time. 'I have a job to do this morning. I said I'd help Dougal with some joinery work. But I'll see you later.'

Waving him off, Kity then put her coat and hat on to pop along to show Minnie her ring before getting on with her working day.

Gordon was filling the front counter of the tea shop with cakes and confectionery when he saw Kity hurrying by, wrapped up against the cold day. He surmised that she was on her way to Minnie's grocery shop to show her the engagement ring.

Minnie sorted her bakery tray with a tempting selection of mincemeat pies, fruit loaf and tattie scones. As the days became colder the demand for bakery items always increased, so she extended her range during the winter.

She'd just added iced buns and doughnuts filled with jam and cream, when Kity came in.

'Oh, let me see your ring.' Minnie's enthusiasm matched Kity's excitement to show her.

Kity extended her hand.

'It's beautiful. Congratulations. I'm so happy for you and Lochlan.'

They were chatting when Pearl came in and joined in the excitement.

Wishes were made on the ring by Minnie and Pearl, and the conversation circled around Kity's plans for the wedding.

'My mind's in a tizzy,' said Kity. 'I never expected Lochlan to propose last night. But he'd set up the house with romantic lighting, candles, dinner and champagne.'

119

Pearl smiled. 'I was hoping for another wedding, but I didn't expect a second Christmas wedding.'

'It's so exciting,' said Minnie.

Kity nodded. 'Lochlan's just given me the bridal magazines. I can't wait to read them, but I wanted to show you the ring before I open up my shop.'

'Gordon and Lochlan both bought bridal magazines here this morning,' Minnie revealed.

'Is Gordon thinking of marrying Eila at Christmastime?' Kity said to Minnie.

'Gordon said that he thought Eila would like the magazines to start planning early for their wedding,' Minnie explained. 'I think Gordon's a wee bit edgy seeing other couples getting married and he's not made any plans with Eila.'

'Do you have any plans yet for your wedding?' Pearl said to Kity.

'Lochlan says that Gordon is happy to make us a cake, and he's offered the tea shop as a venue for our reception,' Kity told them.

'The tea shop?' Minnie exclaimed. 'Oh, lovely.'

'Yes, so we'd have the wedding ceremony at the new house,' said Kity. 'Then a small reception for close friends at the tea shop.'

Continuing to chat about the engagement and wedding plans, Kity finally bought a fresh loaf and milk and headed back to open up her knitting shop.

She put the bridal magazines in the pattern drawer to read later. She needed to get the orders packed and lots of other things done.

Kity had just finished packing the yarn orders and was restocking the shelves when Judy popped in, eager to see Kity's ring and hear all about the romantic proposal.

'We're all excited about a second Christmas wedding,' Judy told her.

'My heart keeps fluttering every time I think about it. I'd no idea that Lochlan was planning to propose last night. I'm still giddy about it.'

'No wonder, especially as you thought you were just going up to see the new house. What's it like by the way?'

'Gorgeous. I love everything about it. The decor is classy but cosy. It feels like home.'

'Well, it's going to be your home soon. I bet that at the mending night tomorrow evening, the ladies will be starting to plan a wedding quilt for you and Lochlan.'

'I don't want to put them to any bother because of us. I know it's short notice.'

'It's a few weeks until the wedding. We've made things in half that time,' Judy assured her. Then she took out the wedding dress sketch book from her bag. 'You said you liked this design. I'd like to offer to make it for you — in chiffon.'

'Oh, Judy, are you sure? You're still working on Poppy's dress.'

'It's nearly finished. And your dress is a design that's easy for me to make. I even have a pattern that I can adapt. I've made variations of this classic pattern before. I'd be happy to make it for you. Eila's dress shop has plenty of white chiffon.'

'Thank you, Judy. I'd love that.' Kity gave Judy a hug.

Judy smiled and tucked the sketch book back in her bag. 'I'll talk to Eila about the fabric and I'll make a start on the dress soon. And you can help. You wanted to learn dressmaking. Well, now is your chance.'

'I'd love to help.'

'I'll need you to come by so I can get your exact measurements for the pattern,' said Judy.

'Yes, I'll pop in.'

Leaving Kity to get on with her knitting work, Judy went back to the bar restaurant to help Jock cook soup and puddings ready for the lunches.

Kity felt even more in a tizzy and couldn't wait to tell Lochlan about her wedding dress plans.

While arranging a new order of yarn on the shelves, a call came through from Eila at the dress shop.

'Can you pop into my shop at lunchtime so I can fit your bridesmaid dress?' Eila said to Kity.

'Yes, I'll be there soon.'

Kity finished restocking the shelves with the lovely new yarn and then locked the knitting shop and went along to the dress shop.

Eila was sitting at her sewing machine and stopped stitching a dress she was working on and went over to a rail where she'd hung Kity's dress. 'I've tacked your bridesmaid dress together, but I'd like you to try it on before I machine the seams. Can you put it on?' She gestured to the small changing room at the back of the shop.

Happy to put it on, Kity was careful not to pull at the seams and stepped out wearing it. 'It looks great and it's a nice fit.'

Eila came over and started to check it. 'I'll take the darts on the bodice in a bit, but apart from that it's ready for machining.'

'You've made a wonderful job of it.'

Eila was pleased. 'I'll push on with making it, then you can come back for another fitting for the length of the hem.'

Kity was as careful to take the dress off as she was to put it on. She handed it back to Eila.

Eila hung it up on the rail. 'Judy was in and told me she's making your wedding dress. How exciting!'

'I'm supposed to be helping her, but I'm sure that Judy will sew most of it.'

'Don't you believe it. Judy will have you cutting the pattern and learning how to put the whole dress together.'

Kity laughed. 'What have a gotten myself into?'

'A whirlwind wedding that everyone's delighted to be part of.' She gave Kity a hug and admired her ring. 'Can I try it on and make a wish?'

'Yes.'

Eila slipped it on, turned it around the required times, closed her eyes and made her wish.

A diamond and sapphire ring from her engagement to Gordon sparkled on Eila's finger.

Kity noticed the bridal magazines sitting on Eila's counter.

Eila shook her head and laughed. 'Gordon gave me these. I sparked the morning reading them.'

Kity nodded. 'I had to put mine in the pattern drawer so I wasn't tempted to keep looking at them instead of getting on with my work.'

'I'd planned to film a new dressmaking video, but I'll film it in the afternoon now.'

Kity looked at the filming area set–up on one part of Eila's sewing table. 'I need something like this for making knitting videos.'

'It's not too fussy. Poppy advised me. She makes lots of embroidery videos. I only make a few of my dressmaking. But she said that having good lighting was important. I bought the stand that holds my phone steady and the two lights online.' She gave Kity a link to the items she'd bought.

They chatted about making the videos, their rings, and plans for the new wedding dress, and then Kity went back to the knitting shop.

Kity ran upstairs and made herself a mug of vegetable soup for a quick lunch, ordered the items that Eila had suggested, and then opened the shop again.

The snow had stopped hours ago, but now snow mist draped itself over the coast and started to blow in towards the shore.

Kity was mesmerised by the wispy view of the sea as she finished packing the orders ready for posting.

Putting her coat on, she headed out to the post office, taking her time so she could admire the snow mist scene. The air had a different quality to it, so still, not even a breeze to waft the haze away.

After handing in the parcels, she walked back to her shop, but paused to take a few photos with her phone of the seascape. She checked the images and nodded to herself. She'd definitely put these on her website for customers to share in the wonderful winter sea view.

Later in the day, Judy was in the grocery shop chatting to Minnie while Bracken snoozed cosy in his basket.

'You're making Kity's wedding dress?' Minnie sounded pleased.

Judy nodded. 'Yes, I'm going to make a start on the pattern. I was in Eila's dress shop earmarking the white chiffon. Eila has put two rolls aside for me, so we've got plenty of fabric. And I've lots of fabric in my own stash. The dress is mainly layers of chiffon on the skirt, a cotton lining and a fitted bodice that I think will look lovely.'

Judy went on to describe the dress design. 'Kity wants to learn dressmaking, so she's going to learn by helping me make her dress.'

'That's a great way to learn,' said Minnie.

'I'm planning to show her how to cut the pattern pieces so she learns the basics.'

'It sounds as if Kity's dress will be a completely different design to Poppy's dress.'

'Yes. Poppy's obviously has more intricate work with the crystals and embroidery, but it suits her. Kity likes the soft chiffon design, so each bride will have their own distinctive style.'

'Is Kity having an engagement party?'

'She probably doesn't have time to organise one,' said Judy. 'I was talking to Jock, and we've got an idea. It's the sewing and mending bee tomorrow night.

Most of the members turn up to the monthly mending, so lots of us will already be there and able to pop next door to the bar restaurant after the bee for a get together. Jock says we can have a wee dance in the function room.'

'Yes, let's do that,' Minnie agreed.

'I'll tell Kity,' said Judy. 'It'll be a fun night.'

CHAPTER NINE

Judy popped into Kity's knitting shop and told her about the impromptu engagement party.

'Tomorrow night!' Kity exclaimed, thrilled but taken aback.

'If you want. Jock and I are happy to organise a wee get together in the function room after the sewing and mending bee night at the tea shop.'

'I hadn't thought about an engagement party. But yes, thank you. I'll tell Lochlan. I'm sure he'll be pleased.'

Judy nodded firmly. 'And remember, drop by when you've time so we can make a start on your wedding dress.'

'I will, Judy.'

Waving, Judy went back to the bar restaurant, leaving Kity thinking what she would wear to the party.

Lochlan had been working on joinery and building tasks for most of the day. In the late afternoon he phoned Kity at the knitting shop.

'I have to work late,' he explained. 'Some folk were caught short by the cold snap, the snow, and need some repairs done to their properties. I wanted to see you tonight, but I'm heading out to a few of the outlying cottages, so I won't be back until later.'

'That's okay,' Kity assured him. 'Do what you have to do. I'm finishing up at the shop soon, but Judy has invited me over to start work on my wedding dress, so I'll do that this evening.'

'Your wedding dress?' He sounded incredulous.

'Yes, Judy's kindly offered to make it for me. I liked one of the wedding dress designs in her sketch book. She wants to start work on it. I'm helping her while learning dressmaking skills.'

'That's wonderful.'

'I know. There's so much that's happened today. I'll tell you all about it when I see you.'

After the phone call, Kity closed up the shop for the night, went upstairs to freshen up, and then headed along to the bar restaurant.

The mist that had hung over the sea for most of the day had cleared. Her breath filtered out into the cold air as she walked along, but the lights from the bar restaurant and the tea shop poured a warm glow over the snow that still covered everything.

The welcoming atmosphere of the bar restaurant pulled her in and she unravelled her scarf, letting it drape around the shoulders of her cream wool coat.She'd freshened her makeup and brushed her light copper hair silky smooth.

Jock spotted her as soon as she walked into the busy bar and waved her over. 'If you're looking for Judy, she's upstairs.' He gestured to her. 'Away up.'

'Thanks, Jock.'

Kity went up the stairs and knocked on the door that was slightly ajar. 'Hello, Judy. It's me. Jock said to come up.'

'Come away in. I'm just working on the pattern for your dress. But we need to get your measurements.'

Judy had her measuring tape draped around her neck.

Kity took her coat and scarf off and chatted while Judy took her measurements and jotted them down.

'Lochlan's working late, so I thought I'd come round. I haven't had a chance to tell him about the engagement party, but I'll explain to him later.'

'Jock says he'll lay on snacks and play plenty of lively dance music. We'll make a night of it.' Judy sounded as excited as Kity felt.

'I'm looking forward to the sewing and mending night too. I've put aside a jumper and cardigan to bring along to demonstrate my mending techniques for knitwear, and a couple of darning mushrooms.'

'I've got one of those in my sewing box. I'll bring mine too. I haven't done much knitwear mending, so I'll be picking up tips from you.'

'I enjoy using contrasting colours to sew the repairs, like colourful patches. Visible mending.'

'I like to use visible mending for repairing some items of clothing like jeans or a denim jacket. I've seen how nice the patches look, as if they're part of the design.'

'I'll show you and any of the other members interested how I do my invisible mending too for knitwear. I know we've exchanged tips at the other mending bee nights, but there are so many ideas to share.'

Judy finished taking the measurements. 'Right, that's those done.' On the table was a file bursting with paper patterns that she'd made over the years. 'I looked through my pattern stash and found the perfect pattern to use for your dress. I'll tweak it where necessary.'

Kity stared at the file overflowing with paper patterns. 'How many do you have?'

Judy laughed. 'I keep all my patterns. These are my bridal and evening wear designs.'

Kity was fascinated to see Judy work.

'There are three pieces for the bodice — two for the back and one for the front,' Judy explained, smoothing them out on her sewing table. 'Then there's the skirt front and back. And facings.'

Kity watched, taking it all in. A roll of the chiffon was stashed nearby. 'Is chiffon difficult to sew?'

'Chiffon has its foibles, but it's one of my favourites so I've learned over the years how to handle it. I use smaller stitches when machining it and rolled hems give a nice finish to the edges. But your dress will need a lining, and we'll make that from a white cotton fabric. Eila has that too.'

Kity's heart started to race thinking about making the dress.

Judy grinned, seemingly enjoying the process. 'It'll all work out beautifully. Trust me.'

Kity calmed her concerns. 'I do. I'm just...'

'Overwhelmed?'

Kity nodded.

'No wonder. A surprise proposal. A Christmas wedding. Planning the reception.'

Kity started to smile. 'Don't forget the impromptu engagement party.'

'And there you were last night at the bee, thinking you were only going to be a bridesmaid at Poppy and Euan's wedding.'

'Bridesmaids!' Kity exclaimed, suddenly wondering if she needed those too.

'We'll be your bridesmaids. The only two differences are — you'll be the bride and Poppy will be one of your bridesmaids. As for the dresses, we've all got nice wee dresses we can wear and I've dresses to lend. We can colour coordinate them or wear a similar style, like tea dresses for example.'

'Yes! Because Gordon said he could lay on a reception at the tea shop. That would be a lovely theme.'

'Well then. That's what we'll do. We'll discuss it with the girls tomorrow night at the mending bee.'

Judy's cheery–calm attitude settled Kity's skittish concerns.

Lifting up a roll of white cotton fabric from her fabric stash, Judy put it on the sewing table. 'Come on, help me lay out the pattern pieces on this cotton so we can start making the toile.'

'A toile?'

'We'll use this light cotton to make a toile, a test version of the dress. That way we won't waste any of the chiffon fabric. I always make a toile so I can perfect my patterns. It seems like extra work, but it's worth doing and I find it saves time in the long run. Fussing and changing a pattern once it's cut is often a lot more work. I prefer to make a test garment.'

Kity helped Judy unroll the white cotton on the cutting table that was set up. 'I keep a roll or two of this in my stash. It's not expensive.'

As Kity learned the process, the time flew in and then they heard Jock trudging up the stairs.

'It's me, ladies. Don't worry, I'm not coming in. I've brought sustenance.'

Judy went over and opened the door and took the tray of tea and sandwiches off of Jock.

'You're a darlin',' Judy said to him.

'The bar's buzzing tonight with folk coming in from the cold,' he told her cheerily and headed back down the stairs.

'Am I keeping you from helping Jock serve the customers?' Kity sounded concerned.

'Nooo, I'm often up here fussing with my dressmaking. We've staff on tonight, so it's fine,' Judy assured her.

Judy draped the toile on to an adjustable dressmaker's mannequin. She pinned and fitted the cotton fabric while showing Kity what she was doing.

'I'm surprised how quickly the dress is taking shape,' said Kity.

'I've been doing this for years and I tend to work fast. Like you're a fast knitter. I'm a fast dressmaker.' Judy stood back to check her handiwork. 'This design is going to work a treat.' Then she put her pin cushion and scissors aside. 'Let's get our tea and sandwiches.'

Lochlan drove his van through the forest. The trees were a mix of evergreens thick with snow and those with bare branches that entwined across parts of the road like a white bridal arch encrusted with snow crystals.

The road led down towards the fields and as he emerged from the forest and drove past the fields he could see the sea glittering in the distance. Euan's flower fields were on one side of the road and there were lights glowing from the farmhouse and Poppy's cottage. A vast winter twilight rested for the night along the coastline. Everything felt still. Nothing to disturb the snow that created a beautiful whiteout over the village.

Kity was on his mind. He thought about stopping and phoning to tell her he'd finished work, but instead he forged on, eager to see her. She'd said she'd be with Judy at the bar restaurant, so he headed there and parked opposite it on the esplanade.

The freezing cold hit him after the cosiness of the van, but he'd been out in the elements for most of the day. The work was done now, so he'd no complaints, and he was looking forward to hugging the breath from his new fiancée. That word had played on his mind all day, making the hours go in quickly. Kity was going to be his wife. What a thought! He couldn't be happier.

The bar restaurant always had a friendly buzz to it, with local folk frequenting it during the day for the bar lunches, but in the evenings it really notched up a gear. It was never raucous, not on Jock's watch, and he was always there, backed most of the time by Judy. That was the type of marriage he hoped for. A couple that had each other's backs.

Music was playing, but there wasn't an event on that evening so the function room was empty, softly lit, biding its time until another night when the dance floor would be bouncing with ceilidh dancing or waltzing.

Lochlan's tall figure wearing a warm, dark jacket turned a few heads. This was the man due to marry Kity. The gossip and congratulations abounded. He glanced around looking for Kity and Judy but there was no sign of them.

'Lochlan!' Jock said, beckoning him to come over to the bar. 'If you're looking for oor lassies, they're dressmaking up the stairs.' Jock motioned above him as he poured a pint of beer for a customer.

'Can I go up?' Lochlan wanted to know.

'Nope. They're secret sewing.' Jock sounded the words in an emphatic whisper.

Lochlan didn't catch on right away what he meant.

'Kity's wedding dress,' Jock clarified.

'Oh, right.' So he wouldn't be able to see Kity after all.

Jock saw the telltale frown on Lochlan's brow. 'You're looking cauldrife the night.'

'I've been working outside for most of the day and tonight.'

'Fancy a bowl of stew to put some heat in your bones?' Jock offered.

'Cheers. I would.'

'Sit yourself down.' Jock indicated a seat at the bar. All the tables were taken.

Lochlan shrugged his jacket off, put it on the back of his bar chair and sat down.

Jock strode off through to the kitchen leaving the two staff to cope with the customers' orders.

Lochlan had barely unwound his thoughts and settled down to relax when Jock reappeared with a bowl of hot stew and a basket lined with a napkin and filled with chunks of thick–cut bread and pats of butter.

'Thanks, Jock.' He tucked in. The flask of tea and pack of sandwiches he'd taken with him in the morning when he'd headed off to work had lasted him all day. He kept thinking he'd be finished each job, but then there was another one, so he'd kept going until he was functioning on the fumes of a cuppa and a cheese sandwich.

Jock took out his phone. 'I'll let Judy know you're here.' Judy picked up. 'Lochlan's downstairs in the bar. I'm feeding him stew and gossip.'

Judy laughed. 'Did you tell him he can't come up?'

'I did, so I'll update him on everything he's missed if that's okay with you and Kity.'

Judy spoke to Kity. 'Lochlan's in the bar looking for you. Jock's feeding him, but he wants to tell him some of the news. Is that okay?'

'Yes, it'll save me from melting his ears with the whirlwind of events,' said Kity.

'Spill the beans on everything, Jock,' Judy told him. 'We'll be a wee while yet. We're making the toile.'

'That sound interesting, complicated and way above my knowledge level. So I'll just let the two of you get on with your secret sewing.' Jock put his phone away and rubbed his hands together. 'So...are you looking forward to your engagement party tomorrow night?'

Lochlan almost splurted out his stew. 'My what?'

'The lassies are having their monthly sewing and mending night at the tea shop tomorrow evening. They'll finish around nine at night, as per usual.'

Lochlan nodded. 'I'm with you so far.'

'Judy and I were thinking that as the ladies were out at night anyway, they could all traipse next door, in here, afterwards and we could have a wee jig to celebrate your engagement.'

Lochlan laughed. 'I go away for a few hours and I come back to a planned engagement party. But that's fantastic.'

'You usually come down to walk Kity home after her bee nights, so just do that, but head in here and we'll kick up our heels. I've got some great music and there isn't an event on in the function room so it's free for us to party.'

Lochlan continued to eat his food, relishing all of it. 'And I didn't expect that Judy would be starting to make a wedding dress for Kity.'

'My Judy doesn't hang around when it comes to dressmaking.'

Lochlan smiled. 'With everything being organised so fast, I'm wracking my brain. I don't think there's much else to sort out.'

Jock leaned on the bar and smiled right at him. 'Oh, I think there is.'

'What?' Lochlan sounded wary.

'Your wedding reception.'

'Gordon's offered to hold that in his tea shop,' Lochlan explained.

'The meal, yes, a late afternoon tea from what I'm told.' Jock shrugged. 'But what about afterwards? I've been thinking, and I mentioned it to Judy, but even Kity doesn't know. We'd like you to have your evening with us. I'll make sure the function room is available. Think of tomorrow night's party as round one.'

Lochlan churned the offer around in his mind and felt his enthusiasm soar. 'Yes, that would be perfect. I thought maybe we'd organise something up at the house, but...' he gestured around him. 'A party night here after the meal at the tea shop would be ideal.'

Jock smiled. 'That's settled then. And now you've got some wedding planning news to tell Kity.'

'Have you any idea about her wedding dress? Is she going to be a traditional bride? Kity's always been full of surprises, including saying yes to marrying me.'

'You didn't hear this from me...I heard them mention lots of white fabric.' He pressed his finger to his lips. 'That's why Judy tells me nothing. I blather it out. But I think Kity is going for her dream dress, so you'd better be dressed to match.'

'I haven't thought what I'd wear.'

'Euan's wearing a suit. But can I suggest you wear a kilt. Not your uncle's one that you borrowed for the ceilidh dancing here recently. A new one for your wedding. There's time to buy one from any of the towns nearby, or even go to Edinburgh. They've all got kilts for sale.'

Lochlan pictured himself standing next to Kity at the wedding wearing a full kilted outfit. He nodded thoughtfully. 'Yes, I think I will.'

Jock grinned. 'And they say that Minnie is the local meddler.'

'I think you and Judy could give Minnie a run for her money, in the nicest possible way.'

As the cheery atmosphere of the bar restaurant wrapped itself around Lochlan, he forgot about the cold, hardworking day. Now all he wanted was to talk about the wedding plans with Kity.

'I'm teaching Euan how to waltz properly for his first dance with Poppy at their reception at the marquee,' Jock told Lochlan. 'They're coming along to the function room a few afternoons to practise. If you and Kity need any help, let me know.'

'I've built in a small dance floor in the living room of my house.'

'You should practise there. Are you light on your feet for waltzing?'

'Not bad, but I could probably do with a bit of polishing my waltz. And brushing up on my ceilidh dancing. If I'm going to wear a kilt to the wedding, I think it's only fitting that there's a mix of dances at our reception party.'

'A man after my own heart. There's nothing like a burl around the dance floor during a ceilidh. I tell you what, tomorrow night at your engagement party, see what you're capable of. I'll help you brush up your skills. Then you can practise on your own wee dance floor at home.'

'We have a plan,' Lochlan said, his smile lighting up his handsome features.

'Maybe it would be a good idea to wear Dougal's kilt again, until you get your own. Then we can see what works for you for the dances.'

Lochlan nodded. 'Smashing idea. Don't tell Kity I'm wearing a kilt. I want it to be a surprise.'

'Bare knees and bare bahookie in this snowy weather. Oh, I think Kity will be impressed.'

'I'm all about impressing Kity, as you know.'

Jock looked thoughtful. 'I've got a great ghillie shirt you can wear with it. The shirt you wore the last time with Dougal's kilt and sporran was fine, but I think we can raise your game for the engagement party.'

'I'm up for that!' Lochlan said, fist bumping Jock and joking around.

'What are you two scallywags laughing about?' Judy said, making her way through the busy bar with Kity in tow.

'You've got your *secret sewing*,' said Jock, sounding mischievous. 'We've got our *scallywag skulduggery*.'

'My money's on us,' Judy said firmly while playing along.

Kity wasn't so sure. 'Lochlan has that glint in his eyes. That blue fire when he's up to something.'

Lochlan grinned at her. 'Blue fire, eh? I never knew I had that effect on you.' He stood up and gave her a warm hug and kiss.

Judy pointed at Jock. 'And you've been stirring up mischief. You've got that meddling look in your eyes.'

Jock hurried round from behind the bar and grabbed his wife in a playful cuddle. 'But you love me for it, don't you?'

Judy giggled. 'More and more as they years go by.'

CHAPTER TEN

Lochlan walked Kity back to the knitting shop from the bar restaurant.

'Jock was wondering if I'm wearing a suit or a kilt for our wedding. What do you think about me wearing a kilt?'

'That would be perfect. You look great in a kilt.'

'A kilt it is then. Would you like to go with me to the shops in Edinburgh? We could make a day of it. Buy our wedding rings while we're there.'

'Yes. I could close the knitting shop on a midweek day,' she suggested, sounding excited.

'Let's do that. We'll get the rings in the morning from a jewellers and then I'll go and buy my kilt. You could have a browse round the shops in Edinburgh while I'm getting kitted out. I'm surmising we're both keeping our outfits a secret from each other until our wedding day.'

'Yes, I'd prefer that. I'll gad about the shops while you're getting your kilt.'

'Then we could have a late lunch.'

They reached the knitting shop and he paused as she opened the door. 'I won't come in as it's late and I've a really early start in the morning.' Pulling her close he kissed her goodnight.

'I'll see you tomorrow night after the sewing and mending bee,' she said.

'Yes, I think there's an engagement party on.'

Kity gazed up at him. 'I didn't expect us to have one, but now I'm so excited.'

'So am I.'

He wrapped her in his arms, kissed her again and then headed away to where he'd parked his van.

Kity stood at the front door and waved as he drove off, and then locked the shop and went upstairs, taking the bridal magazines with her.

Sitting up in bed, she poured through the magazines, looking at the bridal fashion and features about everything from winter bouquets to wedding rings. The latter was of particular interest and gave her ideas for what type of wedding ring would suit her. The winter bouquets were quite beautiful and the colours included Christmas red with berries and vivid greenery to snow white flowers and frosted foliage.

Judy had mentioned when they were making the toile that Euan would be pleased to supply the flowers for her bouquet. But he'd be newly married and she didn't want him to have to fuss with her flowers.

An abundance of thistles growing in Lochlan's garden was certainly something to consider along with white heather and the fresh foliage in her own garden. A Scottish winter theme for her bouquet and buttonhole for Lochlan.

As it was getting late, she knew it was time to sit the magazines aside, put the light off and coorie under the covers to get some sleep.

Lochlan set an early morning alarm on his phone and went to bed. No swimming in the sea for him the next day. He had building jobs to do. Another busy day. Folk were getting their properties repaired, insulated and ready for Christmas. The list of jobs kept piling up, but that was fine. He liked his work and it was helping him establish his business in the village as well as working in the nearby towns.

Pulling the covers around him, he saw that it was snowing. Watching the flakes falling down lulled him to sleep, thinking about Kity, and longing for the time when she would be there with him. Not too long now. Something to look forward to. He'd been wanting to settle down for a while and believed marriage would suit him, especially as it was with Kity, the only girl for him.

Poppy walked across the snow–covered field, blinking against the bright winter sunlight that glinted off the sea as she headed down to the bar restaurant at the shore.

Wrapped up in a warm coat and boots, her chestnut hair was topped with a woolly hat. The craft bag on her shoulder was kitted out with the embroidery thread, needles and other accessories she needed to work on her wedding dress.

She'd planned her day to include embroidering her dress with Judy. Later, she'd attend the sewing and mending bee, followed by Kity and Lochlan's engagement party.

Euan was joining her at the party, and amid all the hectic plans for their wedding, she was happy for them to have a night out together dancing and having fun.

Poppy loved to dance and her outfit for the evening was a dress worn with shoes that she could dance in. No doubt Jock would include ceilidh dances for the party and she was keen to join in with those. She hadn't scheduled the dance lessons with Jock yet, but planned to chat to him about suitable times soon.

She waved to Gordon as she walked by the tea shop and went into the bar restaurant.

'Judy's expecting you,' Jock said cheerily. 'She's up the stairs.'

'Euan and I are going to the engagement party tonight. Maybe we can arrange a time for our first dance lesson.'

'Yes, I'll talk to the two of you tonight and we'll get you started on your waltzing. And I hope you're bringing your dance shoes with you to the party. I'm planning to include plenty of ceilidh dancing.'

'I am, and I'm looking forward to a wee night out with Euan.'

Poppy headed upstairs and found Judy had set up the wedding dress and veil ready for the embroidery work.

'Morning, Poppy. I thought I could work on the bodice while you embroider the veil.'

Taking her coat and hat off, Poppy agreed to Judy's suggestion.

'I've almost finished the crystal and sequin work on the bodice.' Judy showed her the glittering embellishments on the dress.

Poppy gasped. 'It's gorgeous. And you were right about the invisible neckline and the design for the sleeves.'

Judy smiled. 'I'm delighted you're happy with it.'

'But it's so much work for you.'

'I'm in my element when I'm dressmaking.'

Poppy noticed the toile on the mannequin. 'Is that the mock–up of Kity's wedding dress?'

'It is. What do you think?' Judy went over and gestured to the various aspects of the design. 'We're making it in white chiffon. The bodice is fitting but then flows out to a full but soft–flowing skirt. No sleeves, but the neckline and shoulders will have a bit of sparkle on them.'

Poppy joined her for a closer look. 'It's such a classic design and the white chiffon will be wonderful. Quite a fairytale dress.'

'Kity wanted something wispy and dreamlike, and I think this style will suit her.'

'Yes, it will.'

Poppy settled down to start embroidering her veil and they chatted about the dresses.

'Is Kity having any embroidery work on her dress?'

'No.' Judy showed her the design in the sketch book. 'Just a touch of sparkle on the neckline and shoulders.'

'If she changes her mind, tell her I'd be happy to embroider it for her. Even if it's only to sew her name and Lochlan's somewhere on the dress.'

'That's very kind of you, Poppy. I'll tell her.'

'What are you wearing to the engagement party tonight?' said Poppy.

Judy gave an exaggerated sigh and glanced at the wardrobes filled with dresses. 'I don't know. I don't have a thing to wear,' she joked.

'Spoiled for choice more like.'

'You can never have too much of a good thing. And my thing is dresses galore. You're welcome to borrow any you want, unless you've got something of your own.'

'I've got a wee dress that I was going to wear, but...maybe I could be tempted to have a rummage through your wardrobes while I'm here.'

'Help yourself to whatever one you want. And I've told the bee ladies they can do the same. It's all part of the fun.'

'Euan and I have been so steeped in plans for the wedding that I fancy a night out dancing with him. Jock's warned me that he's laying on the ceilidh dances, but that's my thing as you know.'

'Jock's wearing his kilt. So take his warning seriously. He'll be expecting you to show those Scottish dancing skills of yours.'

Poppy spotted a pink dress peeking out from one of the packed rails of garments. She put her embroidery down and went over and lifted it down. 'A sparkly pink cocktail dress!' She glanced round at Judy.

'What can I say. I couldn't resist. I bought it in a bargain vintage fashion design bundle. It's probably only been worn once. I barely had to do anything to it except secure a few of the sequins on the neckline. Try it on, see if it suits you.'

Poppy didn't need any encouragement. She put the dress on and looked at herself in the wardrobe mirror. 'I don't want to outdo Kity. It's her engagement party.'

Judy laughed. 'See that sparkling silver cocktail dress hanging up over there? That's what I've encouraged Kity to wear.'

'You're a bad influence on us girls.'

'I do hope so. And not to be outdone myself, that snazzy blue silk party dress is what I'm wearing. I think we're all needing to go a wee bit wild. With weddings and Christmas and such a busy time of year, let's have some festive fashion fun.'

'The pink cocktail dress it is then.' Poppy took the dress off, hung it up, but planned to take it back with her to the cottage. 'I'll still wear my proper dance shoes.'

'A cocktail ceilidh look will definitely get the party started tonight.'

They were giggling when Jock called up to them. 'Any of you two gigglers wanting tea and a toasted soda scone with cheese or raspberry jam?'

Poppy nodded. 'Cheese for me.'

'Yes, tea and cheesy scones for two please, Jock.'

'Coming right up.'

'The bar smelled delicious this morning,' Poppy remarked. 'It reminded me of the tea shop.'

'Jock's baking one of his bramble and buttercream specials to give Kity and Lochlan an engagement cake. It's a surprise, so don't say anything to anyone.'

'It sounds delicious.'

'He's quite the baker, and he didn't want everything being left up to Gordon. It's two large vanilla sponges layered with buttercream and then decorated with frosting and brambles. Gordon is supplying cupcakes and doughnuts. Pearl is baking a lemon drizzle cake, so we're sorted for tonight's engagement party.'

'What are you taking to the mending bee?' said Poppy.

'A sky blue jumper of mine that's got a bit of wear and tear. Kity says she's going to show me how to mend it. I'm used to repairing clothes, but I'd like to improve my knitwear mending.'

'I have a favourite white cardigan that could do with mending. I'll bring that along. I've repaired a few items before, but there's always something new to learn especially from someone as skilled as Kity.'

Kity worked on finishing knitting Eila's bolero while dealing with the orders for her shop. She updated the news on her website, adding pictures of the sea haze and the snow, along with photos of more new yarn in winter white and cream. And she put balls of Shetland wool aside to knit the jumper for Lochlan.

It snowed during the day and as the evening approached, Kity started to get ready for the sewing and mending bee — and her engagement party.

Judy had dropped off the silver cocktail dress.

Kity looked at herself in the mirror and felt butterflies of excitement as she stepped into her court shoes that had heels she could dance in. She put a soft grey cardigan on over her dress, then shrugged on her coat ready to head along to the tea shop. Her hair hung is soft waves to her shoulders and she braved the cold without a woolly hat. She'd stuffed her craft bag with a selection of colourful yarn scraps to share, knitted items that needed mending and the darning mushrooms. She planned to share her mending tips with the other members and learn handy hints from them.

As she walked by the bar restaurant to head into the tea shop, she saw a notice on the door stating that there was a private party in the function room for invited guests only. Feeling another wave of nervous excitement, she hurried into the warmth of the tea shop and through to where Minnie, Pearl, Judy and the others were getting ready for the bee.

Kity kept her coat on, suddenly feeling overdressed in the silver cocktail dress, but as the ladies took their coats and jackets off to reveal that they'd all dressed up to the nines, she unbuttoned hers and then hung it over the back of her chair.

'Oooh! You look amazing,' Eila said to Kity.

'So do you,' Kity cast right back at her. Eila's dress was aquamarine satin, figure flattering, and from her own shop's collection. She wore her blonde hair down and silky smooth. From the admiring looks she was receiving from Gordon as he served the tea and scones, Eila had chosen the right look for the party.

Poppy came hurrying in unravelling her scarf and taking her coat off to reveal the sparkly pink cocktail dress she was wearing. 'Before you say anything about needing to shield your eyes from the glare of the sequins, let me just blame Judy for tempting Kity and me to dress to dazzle.'

The ladies laughed. And then a few others revealed their party dresses, and suddenly Kity didn't feel overdressed at all.

Minnie smoothed her hands down her dark blue silk dress that had matching sequins around the neckline. 'This dress has been in my wardrobe for ages and never been worn, but Judy told me that sequins were tonight's theme so...'

'It makes me want to ask you to marry me all over again,' a man's voice called through to Minnie. It was her fiancé, Shawn, a tall, strapping farmer in his fifties.

'Och, away you go,' Minnie said, pretending to brush aside his compliment while clearly loving it.

Shawn smiled and sat down in the front of the tea shop preparing to have something to eat and wait until it was time to escort Minnie to the party.

The bee night began with members showing the items they'd brought with them for mending — everything from knitwear to skirts, jackets and quilts.

All helping each other, hints and tips were exchanged along with gossip and updates about the weddings. This included planning to wear tea dresses as Kity's bridesmaids.

Kity had brought a pair of hand–knitted socks with her. 'I knit all my own socks. I haven't bought a pair in years. I use an easy pattern and I love wearing them because I can make them in any colours and types of yarn I want. But, like most socks, the heels wear out, so I thought I'd show you how I mend them. This type of repair can be used to mend the sleeve of a jumper that's worn at the elbows, or a cardigan that's got a wee hole in it.'

Several members wanted to see Kity's technique.

'It's visible mending. I don't try to hide the hole. I make a feature of it. I weave a patch back and forth to mend the damage. I use bright coloured yarn that contrasts with the sock. It jazzes up the mending and I think it looks great.'

While Kity showed them this, and shared the scrap bag of yarn she'd brought, Judy and Poppy practised on the jumper and cardigan they'd brought for mending.

'I love visible mending on fabric too,' said Eila. 'It's the same theory as Kity's patches, only I use embroidery thread to sew the repair. I like to use two or three strands of stranded cotton embroidery thread. I sew running stitches across the hole, weaving different colours of thread to create a visible patch.' Eila demonstrated mending a denim jacket. 'And if there's a tear or a stain I'll satin stitch a motif over it — a flower, butterfly or bee. Make a feature of it.'

Minnie helped one member repair a quilt while advising another member about the quilted cushion cover she'd brought.

'It's a new cushion cover but someone spilt tea on it and I can't get the stain out,' the woman explained. 'Any ideas what I can do to sort it?'

'Hexies are my go–to for mending quilted items,' said Minnie. 'The floral print on the cushion cover would suit having a hexie flower in a ditsy floral fabric sewn on over the mark.'

The woman nodded and went to rummage through the fabric scraps that were on the table to be shared for the mending.

'I have a bag of hexies,' Pearl said, handing the pre–made hexies to the woman. 'There are lots of prints, help yourself.'

'Thanks, Pearl.' The woman selected seven matching–size hexies in printed cotton and began whip stitching and piecing them together into a hexie flower to sew on to the cushion cover as a large, pretty patch.

'Hexies make handy patches for jeans and denim jackets too,' Minnie reminded them. 'You've seen me stitching them on to clothes before. And they're ideal for mending quilted items that are stained or worn.'

As the mending bee evening wore on, the members began to pack up their craft bags and tidy up ready to head next door to the bar restaurant.

A few of their men had started to arrive at the tea shop to accompany them.

Euan arrived and waved through to Poppy.

Gordon was set to join Eila shortly after everyone left and he'd secured the tea shop for the night.

None of the men were wearing kilts, but they'd all dressed smart and tidy.

Kity kept peeking through to see if Lochlan had arrived but there was no sign of him.

'Don't worry,' Judy whispered to Kity, sensing her anxiousness. 'Lochlan will be here.'

No sooner had Judy said this than there was a roaring cheer and clapping from the men at the front of the tea shop as they welcomed Lochlan, congratulated him on his engagement, and seemed to approve that he was wearing a kilt.

'He stole my kilt again,' Dougal told them. 'But the rascal suits it better than me.'

'Oh, I don't know about that,' Lochlan argued lightly. He ran a nervous hand through his dark hair, and his intense blue eyes kept flicking around looking for Kity.

'Lochlan's wearing a kilt and a ghillie shirt,' Poppy whispered to Kity, giving her a nudge.

Kity frowned. 'A ghillie shirt?'

'Yes,' Poppy hissed. 'It's one of those collarless shirts that laces up the front. Some men leave the laces undone a bit so you can see their chest.'

'Lochlan has braved the cold tonight,' Judy chimed-in. 'And there's plenty of his chest on show.'

The men stepped aside and Kity got a glimpse of Lochlan standing there smiling at her. He raised his hand and waved as she nodded back to him. Her heart squeezed just seeing him, taken aback by his sexy looks. He'd worn a kilt before, but that cream shirt did him a lot of favours.

Minnie didn't mince her words. 'Lochlan's looking scorching for you tonight, Kity.'

Kity blushed.

'You've made Kity blush, Lochlan,' Shawn teased him.

Shrugging off the good humoured remarks, Lochlan's heart reacted when he saw Kity wearing the silver cocktail dress. She'd taken her cardigan off and tucked it in her bag. His reaction showed that she'd selected the right dress to wear for their engagement party.

'Shall we?' Lochlan said to Kity, helping her on with her coat and carrying her craft bag for her.

With Lochlan and Kity leading the way, everyone headed out into the snowy night and into the welcoming warmth of the bar restaurant for an evening of fun and celebrations.

Everyone except Gordon and Euan.

Euan hung back to give Gordon a hand carrying the cakes next door while Poppy and Eila were swept away with the bee members.

Euan held a large cardboard box filled with cupcakes and doughnuts while Gordon locked the tea shop.

'How many cakes have you got in here?' Euan pretended it was weighing him down.

'Plenty and a wee bit more,' Gordon told him with a cheery twinkle in his eyes. 'Come on, let's party.'

CHAPTER ELEVEN

Music filtered out of the function room as everyone headed through the bar to enjoy the private party. A buffet was set up in the function room and included cakes, sandwiches, tea and refreshments. Drinks could be purchased from the bar and the dance floor was awaiting the first couples to enjoy the music Jock had for them. He'd selected songs from yesteryear, timeless tunes that suited everything from ceilidh dances to waltzes, along with a popular range to get everyone up dancing.

Jock wore his kilt as he usually did on nights when there was any dancing, making Lochlan and Jock the only two men kilted.

'Put your coats and craft bags over there,' Judy said to the bee members as everyone poured into the function room. A small cloakroom was provided for parties.

'Thanks for letting me borrow this cocktail dress,' Kity told Judy.

'It really suits you, and I see that Lochlan seems happy to have his swagger on.' Judy glanced over to where Lochlan was standing chatting cheerily to guests.

'He's going to wear a kilt for our wedding. A new one. We're heading to Edinburgh to get him kitted out.'

'I love a kilted groom. Suits are smart too, but I think Lochlan in a kilt will be a great look to go with your wedding dress. You'll make a fine couple.'

'Come and cut your cake,' Jock called to Kity and Lochlan. Jock had iced their names on the top of the cake he'd made for them.

'A cake?' Kity gasped.

'Jock baked it himself,' Judy was pleased to tell her.

Kity felt herself welling up at what they'd done to create a wonderful engagement party for them. 'You're so kind.'

Judy gave her a hug. 'It's fun for everyone, and a wee bit special for you two.'

Jock beckoned to Kity and she hurried over and stood beside Lochlan while they posed for photos of them cutting their cake.

Jock snapped a few, as did several others including Minnie.

Euan helped Gordon put the cupcakes and doughnuts on to one of the cake stands on the buffet table while Jock made an announcement.

'Can I ask everyone to grab a glass and raise them in a toast to Kity and Lochlan to celebrate their engagement.' Jock raised his glass to them.

There were cheers all round, the clinking of glasses and plenty of chatter about them getting married before Christmas.

Shawn stood next to Minnie at the side of the dance floor as they ate slices of the engagement cake. 'This reminds me of the night I proposed to you here, and you said yes.'

'It was a great night,' Minnie acknowledged.

'If you fancy getting married to me sooner rather than waiting a while, just say the word,' Shawn told her.

'I'm happy being engaged. It suits me at the moment.'

'Well, just so you know, but I'm happy that you're happy, that's what matters to me,' said Shawn.

Kity ate a piece of her cake as she stood with Lochlan.

'I didn't expect they'd lay on a spread and bake us a cake.' Lochlan sounded genuinely taken aback.

'Neither did I,' Kity mumbled, enjoying the tasty sponge with fresh cream and brambles.

'I phoned one of the kilt shops in Edinburgh and booked an appointment with them for next week,' Lochlan explained. 'They said I can hire a whole kilted outfit, but I'd rather buy one because I've a feeling I'm going to be using it for other party nights here.'

'Yes, you should have a kilt of your own, though you do suit wearing Dougal's.'

'I'm not having it made bespoke, but they said they've plenty of kilts and jackets ready made that I can buy. I had a look at their website and they've got some fine kilts.'

Jock changed the music to a lively beat. 'Let's get this party started with a jig. Take your partners, folks. And that includes you two.' Jock pointed to Kity and Lochlan.

They put their cake down and walked on to the dance floor as other couples partnered up.

Euan held hands with Poppy, and Gordon and Eila were ready to join in.

'We'll kick off with a dance you're all familiar with,' Jock announced. He grabbed Judy and led the charge as the music played.

Pearl was over at the buffet making sure her lemon drizzle cake was on a plate for people to help themselves to a slice when a man spoke over her shoulder.

'Is that lemon drizzle cake?' said Dougal. He wore a dark grey suit, white shirt and tie, and although he wasn't quite as tall as Lochlan, there was a family resemblance and he was a fine figure of a man in his fifties with thick salt and pepper hair and a tidy appearance.

Pearl turned round. 'Yes, I baked it myself.'

'It's my favourite.'

They were no more than local acquaintances and their paths rarely crossed, at least not that Pearl had noticed.

Pearl wore a silky cream dress she'd scooped from one of Judy's wardrobes and had pinned her light auburn hair up in a chignon. Her makeup was soft and flattering and her only jewellery was a pair of diamante earrings from Judy's private emporium.

'You should try a slice,' said Pearl.

'I will but...I was wondering if you'd care to dance with me first.'

Dougal held out his hand to her and she accepted it, and they joined in the dancing.

Kity couldn't stop smiling as Lochlan burled her around. He looked so handsome in his kilt and lace up shirt, and she was even more convinced that he should wear a kilt for their wedding. Though he probably wouldn't be wearing a ghillie shirt, rather a classic shirt and tie with a waistcoat and jacket.

Euan kept admiring Poppy. 'You look gorgeous,' he told her as they danced together.

Poppy smiled up at him as they whirled around.

The lively dance finished and Jock then led Judy into a waltz as the music changed.

'I love this song,' Poppy said to Euan.

'So do I. It's a favourite of mine. I haven't heard it in a while. Want to waltz with me?'

'Yes, let's see how many lessons we'll need from Jock,' Poppy remarked lightly.

As they began to waltz Poppy realised that they danced quite well together, but knew that lessons from Jock would improve their technique.

'How am I doing?' Euan said to her.

'Very well.' Then she became thoughtful. 'This song has the ideal rhythm for a waltz. And it's so romantic.'

They looked at each other for a moment as they danced.

'Are you thinking the same as me?' Euan sounded hopeful.

Poppy nodded. 'This could be the song for our first dance.'

Smiling, they agreed on the music.

'We'll tell Jock later when we arrange a time for our lessons,' Poppy suggested.

Jock and Judy waltzed by them. 'You're both waltzing very nicely,' Jock remarked.

'We'd love this song for our wedding dance,' said Poppy.

Jock winked knowingly and then waltzed on with Judy.

'What are you up to?' Judy said to Jock.

'Ach, I threw in a few classic songs that are perfect for first dance wedding waltzes.'

'You're such an auld romantic.'

Winking again and pulling Judy closer, he waltzed with her and enjoyed the party atmosphere.

'You're looking smashing in that blue dress tonight,' Jock complimented Judy. 'And I see you got the lassies to lavish on the dazzle.'

'Look how Euan's gazing at Poppy.' Judy sounded pleased.

'I'm surprised he can see her without wearing sunglasses,' Jock joked. 'And the same with Kity.'

Judy laughed. 'You're not the only meddler in our house.'

Shawn overheard them as he danced by with Minnie. 'Are you two after Minnie's mischief–making crown?'

'Nah,' said Jock. 'No one can beat Minnie when it comes to meddling and gossip.'

Minnie giggled and then danced away with Shawn.

The dancing continued and then Jock turned the music down slightly to make a suggestion. 'As this is an impromptu party, does anyone fancy throwing caution and decorum oot the windae?'

'What do you have in mind, Jock?' Gordon called to him.

'A samba. Anyone fancy having a go?' Jock jiggled his kilt in readiness.

'No, Jock,' Judy hissed. 'You're wearing a kilt.'

'All the better for waggling in.' He demonstrated a samba move. 'It's all in the bounce action. Bounce and move, bounce and step. Let yourself go and feel the rhythm.'

Judy was about to curtail Jock's plan when she noticed that several of the couples were having a go, trying to replicate the bounce motion. Including Poppy and Euan. Poppy seemed to know the samba and Euan took her lead.

Lochlan was well up for it, feeling his kilt helped rather than hindered the bouncing motion.

Kity joined in with Lochlan, trying not to laugh.

As several couples gave it a go, Judy kept her sensible remarks to herself and allowed Jock to take her hand and dance the samba with him.

The music, laughter and cheerful voices of the guests rose up, filling the night with fun among friends all there to celebrate the engagement.

'Oh Minnie, you were made for the samba,' Shawn told her, grinning.

She was enjoying herself. 'I haven't danced it in years, but I remember the rhythm.'

'I don't know if I'm doing it right, but lead the way,' said Shawn.

'What's next, Jock, a tango?' Gordon shouted over to him jokingly.

'Don't encourage him, Gordon,' Judy called back, while everyone continued to have fun.

A few dances on, Jock announced, 'I'm going to invite Poppy to give us one of her excellent Scottish Highland dance displays.'

Guests clapped encouragement.

Poppy stood next to Euan, blushing slightly, unsure whether to step up. 'It's Kity and Lochlan's night.'

'I know,' said Jock. 'But we're all looking forward to the two weddings. It's like having three Christmases to celebrate this year.'

As the guests further encouraged Poppy, she stepped into the middle of the dance floor. 'I'm not really dressed for Highland dancing.' She gestured to her pink sequin cocktail dress, though she was wearing her dancing shoes.

Jock spoke up. 'I'm reliably informed by my dear wife that your outfit tonight is a *cocktail ceilidh* look.'

Poppy laughed and the guests appreciated the light banter.

'Okay, I'll give it a go, Jock,' Poppy agreed.

Jock started the music and Poppy began dancing, displaying her years of training, skirling and spinning across the floor in time to the lively tune.

It was only when she spun around towards the doorway leading on to the main bar that she realised people were peering in to enjoy her dancing display. Without missing a beat, she continued on, and by the end of the dance the party guests and onlookers from the bar were cheering and clapping in time with her.

'Thank you, Poppy,' Jock announced. 'I think she's put us in the mood for some ceilidh dancing ourselves.' He changed the music to suit a Scottish reel and the dance floor filled up with guests eager to give it a go.

'And can I just remind you that there are plenty of refreshments over at the buffet,' Jock added. 'That big jug of what looks like blue lemonade is one of my cocktail concoctions. There's a reason for the wee glasses beside it. Go easy on it. It's strong stuff. A mix that will blaw yer knickers aff.'

No one except Dougal seemed to have touched a drop of it, but with Jock's pitch about its potency, a few people were keen to have a glass.

Kity and Lochlan took a break as the dancing continued.

'Dougal seems very taken with Pearl tonight,' Kity observed. 'He's danced with her a few times this evening.'

'He does,' Lochlan agreed. 'But he's had glasses of Jock's special cocktail. I think he's a wee bit blootered now.'

Kity laughed. 'Pearl seems happy dancing with him.'

Lochlan agreed with that too.

As Dougal and Pearl walked off the dance floor, Lochlan hurried over and spoke to his uncle as Kity went to talk to Pearl.

'You and Pearl are having fun this evening,' Lochlan remarked.

'Yes, she's going to bake a lemon drizzle cake for me. And come round the house one day to show me her baking techniques,' said Dougal.

Lochlan tried to hide his surprise.

'Don't give me that look,' Dougal said, trying not to smile. 'You're not the only one in our family to fancy a lass from afar.'

'You've got a secret fancy for Pearl? You never mentioned it.'

'That's why it's called a secret crush.' Dougal shook his head trying to knock some sense into himself. 'I'm blabbering because of those cocktails.'

'Tell me more,' Lochlan encouraged him.

Dougal glanced around making sure he couldn't be overheard. 'I've liked Pearl for a while now. I've seen her around the village, but I never had the nerve to do anything about it. Besides, I've been on my own since the divorce. You were only a boy then. I'm set in my ways, but...well, having you home to stay while my arm mended reminded me how nice it is to have company. Now that you're in your own house, and have been for a while, despite not telling Kity what you were up to, I've felt sometimes that I'm rattling around in my house on my own too often.'

'So you're thinking of getting serious with Pearl?'

Dougal shrugged. 'No, I'm just thinking it would be nice to have someone to enjoy a meal out with some evenings, or to partner up with for nights like this. A wee friendship understanding.'

'With potential?'

'That would be up to Pearl. Or we'll just keep it nice and friendly which is fine. But I've long thought that she's a lovely woman. Before Minnie started dating Shawn I thought she was nice, but she's far too wild for the likes of me. Pearl on the other hand is more settled.'

'You think Minnie is wild!' Lochlan spoke louder than he'd intended, and Minnie overheard and glanced over at him.

Dougal tried not to laugh as Minnie stared at Lochlan, waiting on an explanation.

'Wild about Shawn,' Lochlan lied, calling over to her.

Minnie nodded that she agreed and squeezed Shawn's arm.

'Phew!' Lochlan whispered to his uncle, causing Dougal to guffaw. 'I need a glass of Jock's cocktail.'

'No you don't. Keep a clear head for Kity. Enjoy your engagement party.'

Lochlan took Dougal's advice and poured himself a glass of iced lemonade and one for Kity. He took it over to her.

Pearl peeled away from Kity and once again teamed up with Dougal for the dancing.

'Is there a romance brewing?' Kity said taking a sip of the lemonade Lochlan gave her.

Lochlan downed half of his drink. 'Brewing and on the boil.'

Kity smiled, and looked around her. 'This will be a great venue for our wedding reception evening party.'

'It will.' Lochlan put their drinks aside, pulled her close and gave her a loving kiss.

Jock hounded them playfully. 'We'll have less canoodling and more dancing.'

Laughing, Lochlan and Kity joined in with the others on the dance floor.

As one lively jig finished, Jock changed the mood to a slower–paced waltz. The twinkle lights decorating the function room added to the romantic ambiance.

Poppy attempted to improve Euan's technique, showing him the rise and fall movement and encouraging him to dance smoothly.

'The function room is free tomorrow afternoon if the pair of you are interested,' Jock said, dancing over to them with Judy.

Poppy nodded up at Euan, hoping he'd agree.

'Yes,' said Euan. 'Shall we say around two–thirty?'

'I'll see you both then. We'll practise for about an hour,' Jock told them. 'And I'll have your song ready for playing. And a couple of alternatives.'

'Thanks, Jock,' Poppy said as he waltzed away with Judy.

'That's handy for me,' Poppy told Euan. 'I'd planned to work with Judy on my wedding dress, so I'll do that after our dancing.'

'And I'll head back up to the farmhouse so you won't have to hide any of your sewing from me,' Euan assured her.

Gordon and Eila were at the buffet. He poured her a cup of tea.

The doughnuts he'd made were gone, as was the engagement cake and the lemon drizzle cake, leaving only a few cupcakes and some sandwiches.

'Folk have been enjoying the baking tonight,' said Gordon. 'I thought I'd over–baked, but I'm glad that everything's been popular.'

Eila bit into a cupcake and nodded.

Gordon laughed.

Eila took a sip of her tea. 'I've been reading about wedding buffets in the magazines. Thanks for buying them for me.'

'I've got other magazines on order at Minnie's shop. I'll check tomorrow to see if they're in.'

'I'm going to make my own wedding dress, but I love seeing the different styles in the features.'

'Take your partners for the last ceilidh dance of the night,' Jock announced. 'Followed by a slow dance to end what has been a wonderful evening. And congratulations again to Kity and Lochlan.'

Guests gave another cheer and round of applause to the happy couple, and then partnered up for the dancing.

Eila took another quick sip of her tea, and giggled as Gordon grabbed her hand and hurried her over to join in the ceilidh fun.

After the extra lively burling and twirling, couples seemed ready to slow dance under the dimmed lighting.

Kity and Poppy's cocktail dresses sparkled under the glow and highlighted the two brides–to–be dancing with Lochlan and Euan.

Jock stood with Judy at the side of the room. He held his phone up and filmed several minutes of the final slow dance.

'Make sure you get everyone in,' Judy advised him.

Jock adjusted his stance so he could capture all the couples together on a night they'd long remember.

After the party, Lochlan helped Kity on with her coat and they stepped outside the bar restaurant. Snow was on the ground and he lifted her up in his arms and carried her along to the knitting shop.

Kity giggled and held on to her craft bag — and Lochlan.

'What a great night we had,' she said.

'It was,' he agreed, carrying her as if it was no effort across the snow–covered esplanade.

As they reached the shop Kity expected him to put her down, but instead he insisted she used her key to open the door while he was still holding her.

Laughing, she opened it. 'You can put me down now.'

He stepped inside still holding her for a moment.

'What are you doing?' she said, smiling.

'I'm practising for when I carry you over the threshold after our wedding. Our engagement party night is a good time to see how it feels.'

He then put her down gently. The shop was lit only by a few twinkle lights in the window display. The shimmering sea and snow created a magical quality to the night's glow, and as Lochlan kissed her goodnight she pictured what it would be like when they were married.

'I'm driving Dougal home as he's happily tipsy and I'll drop Pearl off at her house too,' he explained. 'But I thought I'd come by tomorrow and put the lantern up on the outside of your shed.'

'Yes, I'm expecting a delivery of items so that I can set up my shed to film my knitting videos. Eila showed me her set–up and said that having adequate lighting was important.'

'I have plenty of extra lights that I can put up inside your shed if you want,' he offered.

'Great. I'll see you tomorrow then.' She put her bag down, wrapped her arms around his neck and kissed him.

Smiling, he walked away, and she peered out the front door watching her kilted heartthrob stride back to the bar restaurant to pick up Dougal and Pearl.

A message came through on her phone, and she saw that Jock had sent her a copy of the video from the party, plus several photos of her and Lochlan cutting their cake. Closing the shop door, she stood in the glow of the twinkle lights and watched the video of the dancing. And there she was with Lochlan. Her heart ached seeing him dancing with her, looking so sexy and handsome in his kilt.

Tucking her phone in her pocket, she lifted her craft bag and headed upstairs to bed.

Feeling the tiredness of the busy day and a dance–filled night, she snuggled under the covers and fell asleep.

CHAPTER TWELVE

Lochlan finished putting the lantern up outside the door of Kity's shed. It glowed in the pale grey morning light. The shed was encrusted with frost and the roof was iced with snow.

Kity stepped out of the warmth of the shed. She'd switched the heater on while she'd assembled the set–up for filming her knitting videos. Lochlan had arrived as she was adjusting the flexible arm that held her phone above her work area and had tightened the bracket that secured it in place. Despite it being cosy inside, the exterior remained frosty.

'The lantern looks so pretty.' Kity's breath filtered into the crisp, cold air. The garden was once again covered with overnight snow. She'd layered herself up for warmth in a thermal top under her Fair Isle jumper to tackle the task of setting up her makeshift craft studio.

'You're freezing,' he said. 'Come on, let's get you out of the cold.'

'It's just so cosy in the shed that it feels icy in the garden.'

'I'll check the spotlights are working okay before I go.' He stepped into the shed and Kity followed him, closing the door to keep the heat in. 'Sit as if you're demonstrating your knitting so I can adjust the lights.'

Kity sat down at her work table, pressed the record button on her phone, and pretended to be knitting.

Lochlan peered at her phone, noticing that one of the spotlights needed tweaked so that the area was lit.

'There you go, that should show your knitting to full advantage.'

'I appreciate you helping me.'

'You had this up and running yourself. I only added the spotlights.'

She smiled at him giving her the credit.

'What are you going to be knitting for your video?' He saw the colourful yarn and knitting needles ready for the demonstration.

'Socks. I thought customers would like to see how to knit their own socks using two straight needles. Knitting them flat rather than in the round. It's fairly easy once you get the hang of it. And I'm going to show them that you can knit them with scraps of various coloured yarn. It's a great way to use up spare balls of yarn to create an artistic and fun look to the socks.'

'That sounds like a great idea.' He buttoned his jacket up, lifted his tool bag and stepped out into the snowy garden. 'I'll leave you to get on with your knitting, and see you later.'

Kity followed him out and then frowned as he walked down to the bottom of the garden. A hedge separated her garden from one of Euan's flower fields.

'Where are you going?'

'I'm taking a shortcut back up to the house. I walked down to get some fresh air.' His long legs cleared the hedge with ease.

Kity hugged her arms around her. 'There's plenty of fresh air this morning.' A light breeze blew in from the sea bringing a sharp saltiness that mingled with the winter greenery in her garden and the earthy scents of the surrounding fields.

'I'm helping Jock with a secret job late this afternoon once he's finished Poppy and Euan's dance lesson. But maybe we could have dinner tonight,' said Lochlan.

'A secret job? What is it?'

'I promised Jock I wouldn't tell anyone. He's planning a grand gesture. That's all I can tell you.'

'Hmmm, that sounds intriguing.' She smiled sweetly. 'Can't you give me a little hint?'

'Nope, but don't panic when you see what we're up to.' Grinning teasingly, he started to walk away across the snow–covered field.

'What do you mean don't panic?' she called after him.

Lochlan kept on walking, and raised his hand in a casual wave without glancing back.

Kity was sure she saw his shoulders judder trying to suppress his laughter.

'Rascal,' she muttered, and then went back into her shed.

A note on the door of her shop read: *I'm in the garden shed if you're looking for me.*

She proceeded to film herself casting on the required amount of stitches to knit socks. Explaining everything from the type of worsted yarn she was using to the size of needles, she demonstrated each aspect of her pattern.

During the morning she continued to knit one of the socks, pausing a couple of times to deal with customers in her shop, and then popping back out to the shed to film the knitting.

Poppy and Euan partnered up for their first waltz lesson mid–afternoon in the function room.

Judy and one of the staff attended to customers in the bar restaurant, allowing Jock to tutor them without interruption or prying eyes. The doors leading from the bar to the function room were closed.

Poppy wore her dancing shoes and a full–length dress that Judy insisted she wear so Euan would learn how to navigate his waltzing while she was wearing her wedding dress. The evening dress wasn't the same style as her bridal design, but it had a long, silky skirt that mimicked her wedding dress quite well.

'I know you said you liked this song.' Jock put the music on to play. 'But I have two other choices in case you want to try waltzing to those.'

'What do you want me to do first?' Euan said to Jock, ready to follow his instructions. He'd worn a smart suit, shirt and tie and brogues, a match for the type of wedding attire he'd be wearing when they were dancing at the reception.

'Take Poppy in hold,' Jock instructed. He adjusted Euan's hands and shoulders.

Poppy smiled at Euan, ready to begin.

'Remember,' Jock reminded them. 'All eyes will be on the pair of you, so keep your posture upright but not uptight. You want to look poised without posing.'

Euan felt a sense of trepidation. Everyone would be watching them. What if he messed up?

'Relax,' Jock told him, reading the frantic frown etched across Euan's brow. 'I'll have you ready to sweep your lovely bride across the dance floor in the marquee. I'm assuming it'll be the same type of dance area we usually have in the marquee party nights.'

'Yes,' said Euan. 'The set–up will be as usual. We've had plenty of parties in my field over the years. It'll be like that, only this will be our wedding reception.'

It was Poppy's turn to feel a pang of trepidation.

'Poppy will keep you right,' Jock assured Euan, not picking up on Poppy's puckered brow.

Poppy glanced around estimating the size of the function room. 'Will the dance floor in the marquee be a lot bigger than this?'

Jock thought about this. 'A bit bigger, but don't let that phase you. You don't need to use the whole floor at the marquee. You want to be the focus of the first dance. Practising here is ideal. When you're in the marquee, you can sweep around the middle and that will leave room for other couples to join you.'

'The marquee has plenty of room around the edges for people to watch the dancing and enjoy the buffet too,' Euan explained to Poppy.

She found herself smiling while her heart raced with excitement.

'Okay, let's get you pair waltzing like pros.' Jock turned the music up slightly and Poppy and Euan started to dance.

Jock had watched them carefully at the engagement party and decided to skip the basics as

Euan had mastered the waltzing technique quite well. He just needed fine tuning.

Jock rewound the song back to the start. 'Use the introduction to the song to make a bold statement that you're waltzing off into the night.'

Euan listened to the beat, realising it was strong and steady, so he took Jock's advice and listened to the music as his lead. 'Once I get started I'm okay.'

'Let Euan take the lead, Poppy. That's it,' said Jock.

Judy smiled to herself as she worked in the bar. She could hear the music filtering through from the function room along with Jock's kind but commanding instructions. Poppy and Euan were in capable hands.

Lochlan came striding into the bar carrying a piece of equipment. He walked right up to Judy.

'This is the air pump Jock wanted.' Lochlan held it up, thinking she'd tell him to put it through in the store cupboard.

Judy stopped polishing the whisky glasses. 'What does Jock want a big air pump for?'

A clutch of realisation gripped Lochlan. 'Oh, eh...nothing. I'll away and...sort things out.' He started to hurry towards the door.

'Lochlan!' Judy called after him. 'Is there something going on?'

'No, nothing,' Lochlan lied, wishing he'd brought the pump later when he was due to help Jock with the job they'd planned.

Judy's suspicions were aroused. Jock was up to mischief. She glanced at the function room door, tempted to pop her head in and ask him what he was planning, but she didn't want to spoil the dance lesson.

'A lemonade shandy, please Judy,' a customer ordered.

Another customer smiled hopefully as he approached her while she poured the beer and lemonade drink. 'Is there any apple pie and custard left?'

Judy tended to the customers and put her suspicions on hold, for the moment.

Jock used his phone to film Poppy and Euan waltzing around the dance floor.

When the music finished, they came over to view their waltzing.

'I can see where I'm going wrong,' said Euan. 'You're right about my posture. I need to keep my shoulders back.'

'You're doing really well, Euan,' Poppy told him. 'You just need to practise. We both do.'

'Two more lessons should be adequate,' said Jock. 'Let's get you dancing again now that you've seen yourselves together.'

Heading back to the middle of the floor, Euan took Poppy in hold and Jock started the music. 'Remember, posture and position — that's it, nice and smooth with your rise and fall.'

Customers kept Judy busy in the bar while the lesson continued. Chatting to customers, the time went in, and then the music in the function room stopped.

Jock opened the doors and Judy saw the smiling faces of Poppy and Euan chatting excitedly about their first lesson.

Judy went in to talk to them. 'How did it go?'

'Very well,' Poppy said, beaming at Euan. 'Jock thinks we only need another two lessons and we'll be ready for dancing at the wedding.'

Jock showed Judy a clip of them dancing. 'They look like a fine couple.'

Judy watched them waltzing and nodded. 'The two of you dance well together.'

'Thanks for letting me use one of your dresses. I'll pop upstairs and get changed, but I think I'll need a hand with the zip,' Poppy said to Judy.

'Come on, let's get you changed.' Judy led the way upstairs. 'And are you staying a wee while to work on the embroidery for your wedding dress?'

'Yes,' said Poppy, and then she smiled at Euan. 'I'll see you later as planned.'

Euan nodded happily.

Jock checked the time. 'Lochlan should be here soon, but can I offer you a cuppa before you go, Euan?'

'Eh, yes, I could do with a tea. Though I have to say I enjoyed the dance lesson.'

Jock and Euan walked through to the bar.

'Your choice of song is great,' said Jock, heading behind the bar to make the tea.

Euan sat down at the bar. 'I liked the other two songs you played as well, but we're definitely going to stick with the first one.'

'I'd be happy to sort out your music for the wedding reception,' Jock offered.

'That would be wonderful. If you're sure it's not too much bother.'

Jock served up the tea. 'Nae bother. I'm in my element compiling play lists.'

'I'll tell Poppy to tick box another task off her to–do list.'

They were chatting when Lochlan came in, cautiously glancing around to see if Judy was there.

'Are you being hunted?' Jock joked with Lochlan.

'No, but I messed up earlier. I came in with the air pump and aroused Judy's suspicions,' Lochlan explained.

Jock's smile turned to concern. 'Right, we'd better get started while she's busy upstairs with Poppy.'

Euan took a sip of his tea. 'What skulduggery are you two up to?'

One of the bar staff overheard and glanced at them.

'Wheesht!' Jock whispered to Euan, urging him to be quiet. 'I'm planning something special, but Judy gets worked up when I do anything...adventurous.'

Euan kept his voice down. 'Can I help?'

Lochlan looked at Jock and nodded.

Jock leaned close and confided to Euan. 'The fairy lights are in a fankle. Could you unravel them while Lochlan and I blow up Santa?'

Euan jokingly checked his tea. 'Is there something in this or am I just hallucinating? What are you up to with Santa?'

'Swally your tea down and come through to the kitchen store cupboard.' Jock beckoned Euan to follow him.

Lochlan had the air pump hidden in his work bag and went with them.

178

The three of them disappeared into the large store cupboard and Jock revealed his daring plan.

'Judy!' Poppy called to her. 'Come and have a keek out the window. I just saw Jock climbing up a ladder outside the building.'

'What!' Judy exclaimed and ran over to peer out the window. 'Is that an inflatable Santa Claus?'

'No, it was definitely Jock,' Poppy insisted.

Judy shook her head. 'No, come and see for yourself.' She blinked. 'And what is Lochlan doing climbing up too with fairy lights wrapped around his shoulder?'

Poppy had been sitting embroidering her wedding dress and put it aside to hurry over to the window. Peering down she saw Euan standing at the bottom of the ladder keeping it secure while Jock and Lochlan climbed up it.

'What are they playing at?' Judy gasped, ran out of the room and dashed downstairs.

Poppy ran after her.

Outside they encountered Euan footing the ladder.

'Jock, what are you lot doing?' Judy shouted up to him.

'Just putting the Christmas decorations up, Judy.'

'Be careful up there you silly sausage!'

'We'll have Santa and the lights up in a jiffy,' Jock called down to her. 'Away in out of the cold.'

'I'm standing right here until you're safely back down,' said Judy. 'And don't you dare climb up on that roof.'

'I won't,' Jock told her. But Lochlan would.

179

Hoisting himself up on to the flat area of the bar restaurant rooftop, Lochlan lashed the inflatable Santa to the railing as planned. Then he started to unravel the fairy lights, handing Jock one end to secure to the outside of the building.

Poppy clasped the neck of her jumper. 'I can't look,' she said while watching everything they did.

By now, customers had come out to watch the spectacle.

Kity was on her way back from the post office to her knitting shop and saw the small crowd gathered outside the bar restaurant. Then she glanced up and gasped. 'Lochlan!'

Her voice was blown away in the cold sea breeze and he didn't hear her. She knew his building work required him to climb up for some of the construction, but seeing him draping fairy lights along the top of the bar restaurant made her stomach flip. Of course, he looked secure, but she couldn't help but hold her breath as she watched the festive furore.

Jock started to climb down the ladder as Lochlan finished tying the fairy lights up.

Both men climbed back down.

'You silly auld fool!' Judy scolded Jock, but wrapped him in a cuddle of relief. 'Don't do things like that.'

'Oi! Less of the auld. I'm a man in my prime and fit as a fiddle,' Jock said jokingly.

Kity hurried over to Lochlan. 'I didn't expect to see you up on the roof. Is this what you were secretly planning with Jock?'

Lochlan nodded. 'We knew we could do it fine and safe, but Jock didn't want Judy getting worked up,' he whispered.

Kity hugged him, and then Euan helped Lochlan carry the ladder to his van.

Poppy shook her head at Euan.

Euan held his hands up. 'I was only helping to foot the ladder so it didn't shoogle.'

'Come on in for a cuppa,' Jock beckoned to them.

All of them, including Kity, went into the bar restaurant.

While Judy made the tea, Jock and Lochlan went through to the electrical power box in the kitchen.

'All set,' Lochlan confirmed, checking that the power was connected.

Jock went back through to the bar.

'Everyone outside for the Christmas lighting,' Jock announced, shooing them out to stand in front of the bar restaurant ready for Lochlan to switch them on.

Judy linked her arm through Jock's, Euan put his arm around Poppy's shoulder and they all gazed up.

A twilight sky arched above them, and as the colourful fairy lights lit up, they all cheered.

Lochlan ran out to see their handiwork and join Kity. The reaction from the onlookers confirmed they liked the decorations.

Gordon came hurrying out of the tea shop and gazed up at the fairy lights. 'And you've got a Santa on the roof!' He laughed. 'How did you manage that, Jock?'

Jock thumbed at Lochlan.

'I'd better get my Christmas decorations up soon.' Gordon went back inside his tea shop and everyone else followed Jock to get a warming cup of tea at the bar.

Gordon took a tray of fruit scones out of the oven, and then started to pipe buttercream on a batch of cupcakes. But he was itching to check his Christmas decorations.

Putting the piping bag aside, he opened the kitchen store cupboard and reached up to a top shelf where he'd stashed boxes of his decorations. Pulling down the box marked fairy lights, he looked at the tangle and sighed.

'Any chance of a pot of tea and two cheese pastries please, Gordon?' A customer called into the kitchen.

'Coming right up,' Gordon assured them, prying himself away from planning the tea shop illuminations. Not that he wanted to compete with Jock. He just liked Christmas, and as one of the businesses had put their decorations up, the rest would follow. The tea shop in the past few years had looked lovely lit up. Now that he'd refreshed the colour scheme and added a new pink theme canopy, he was eager to highlight it with plenty of colourful Christmas lights.

Next door, the chatter in the bar restaurant circled around Poppy and Euan's dance lesson.

'I'm not going to show you what I filmed,' Jock told the others. 'I want their dance to be first seen at their wedding reception. But I can say that they did well today.'

Encouraged by this, Kity and Lochlan agreed on a time for a lesson from Jock.

Two customers came in from the cold brushing snow from their jackets. 'That's the snow on again,' one of them announced.

'Do you fancy having dinner here?' Lochlan suggested to Kity.

Kity nodded. 'Yes, it's nice and cosy, and whatever's cooking in the kitchen smells delicious.'

'It's our traditional stew.' Jock handed them a menu. 'Served with tatties, vegetables and bread.'

Lochlan noticed Poppy exchanging a glance with Euan. 'Would you like to join us?' Lochlan offered.

Poppy and Euan were happy to accept.

The foursome moved over to one of the tables ready to have dinner together. The conversation was all about their forthcoming weddings and the plans they were making.

Judy set up plates in the kitchen and Jock used a large ladle to serve up four stew orders.

'I quite fancy this for my dinner tonight.' Judy scooped mashed potatoes on to the side of the plates.

Jock added a helping of mixed vegetables to the orders. 'Anything else you fancy?'

Judy lifted two plates up and gave him a knowing smile.

'Does that mean I'm in the good books again after my antics with the decorations?'

'I suppose so,' she joked with him and carried the plates through to serve to Kity and Lochlan.

Jock grinned to himself and lifted the other two plates for Poppy and Euan.

Leaving the foursome to enjoy their dinner, Jock made another plate of stew and sat Judy down at their private table in the corner of the kitchen. 'Get that down you. I'll join you in a minute once I catch up on the orders.'

CHAPTER THIRTEEN

Gordon tidied up the tea shop after the last of the customers left for the night. He carried the boxes of Christmas decorations through to the front of the tea shop, eager to get his fairy lights up.

Unravelling the sets of coloured lights, he brought his stepladder through from the kitchen and carried it outside. He climbed up and began to drape a set of lights along the edge of the canopy.

The buzz from the bar restaurant resonated out into the cold night air. The snow had stopped again, but a few stray flakes fluttered down.

Gordon was in his shirt sleeves, but he knew it wouldn't take him long to pin the lights up outside the tea shop.

Climbing down, Gordon switched the lights on and then stood admiring his handiwork. He nodded to himself. Very Christmassy.

Carrying the ladder back into the kitchen, he decorated the inside of the front windows and doorway with lights, enjoying the heat from the fire still aglow.

He checked the time. Eila had called earlier to say she was working late to finish a dress order for a customer that needed to be posted out the next morning. This was handy, because he wanted to surprise her with his light display. She was probably due to arrive soon.

Adding baubles, tinsel and ornaments to the tea shop windows, he went out to have a look at the display.

'Gordon,' Eila called to him as she locked up her dress shop.

He waved to her and waited while she hurried along towards him. She wore a warm jumper and jeans, but she hadn't bothered wearing a coat thinking she was only popping to the tea shop.

From her surprised and delighted expression, she'd been so steeped in work she didn't know about the decorations being up outside the bar restaurant or the tea shop and put a spurt on to join Gordon.

'Wow! Christmas has arrived!' She was particularly impressed with the fairy lights adorning Gordon's premises. 'The tea shop looks so Christmassy.'

His thoughts exactly, except...one end of the lights wasn't tied securely.

'I'll get the ladder from the kitchen,' he said, trying to reach up to sort it, but it was just out of his grasp.

'You don't need the ladder,' Eila said excitedly. 'Lift me up. I'll tie it.'

'Okay, climb on to my shoulders.' Gordon crouched down so she could climb on.

'I just meant lift me up, but...all right...if you're sure.'

Gordon patted his shoulders. 'Come on, it's freezing out here.'

Giggling caused her to wobble while sitting balancing on his strong shoulders.

Gordon stood up with more ease than she'd anticipated, though she knew he was fit and strong from his swimming and hard work.

Balancing Eila on his shoulders, Gordon stepped closer so she could reach the dangling fairy lights.

Unknown to them, Judy was now outside the bar restaurant, standing back on the esplanade to capture a picture of Santa and the festive lights high up on the building to update their website.

Gordon and Eila were so wrapped up in the fun of the moment that they didn't notice her.

Smiling to herself at their happy antics, Judy snapped a picture of them, along with the bar restaurant display, and then went back inside without them even noticing her.

Eila reached up to full stretch. 'I've nearly got it. There, that's it. It won't dangle again.'

Gordon stepped back, keeping Eila on his shoulders, and admired the fairy lights.

'You can put me down now,' she said, laughing, knowing he was fooling around with her.

'I think I'll keep you here for a wee bit.' Gordon twirled around.

'Gordon!' Eila shrieked with laughter. 'You're a rascal.'

'Bend your head, we're going inside.' He walked towards the front door and Eila leaned down so he could walk through with her into the warmth of the tea shop.

He gently lowered her down and helped her alight from where she'd been perched on his shoulders.

She swiped at him playfully. 'That was fun, but you're still a rascal.'

'Can I make it up to you with a cup of hot chocolate and buttered toast?'

Eila pretended to consider this. 'Okay, I suppose so. But only if you add extra sprinkles to my hot chocolate.'

'Consider it done.'

They went through to the kitchen and Eila rummaged through a box of decorations he'd kept aside. 'These baubles are so pretty. Where are you going to put them? Do you have a Christmas tree?'

'Yes, I've put it upstairs in the living room front window. I thought we could decorate it together.'

'Our first Christmas decorating a tree.' The delight in her voice made his heart melt.

While Eila organised the baubles and a set of colourful lights, Gordon made the hot chocolate and toast. He carried it upstairs on a tray, having dimmed the tea shop lights to a nightglow. The fairy lights in the windows cast a warmth out on to the snow–covered esplanade.

'Do you want to hang the first bauble on the tree?' Eila said after munching a slice of toast washed down with hot chocolate.

'We'll hang one each,' he suggested, loving her enthusiasm as she decided to begin with a shiny red bauble and handed him a gold one.

'Here's to our first Christmas,' she said, hanging her bauble on a branch.

'And to many more.' Gordon hung his bauble next to hers, causing her to lean over and kiss him.

A message popped up on Eila's phone. 'Judy saw our antics outside the tea shop.' She smiled and held the phone up to show him the picture Judy had sent them.

'Make sure to send a copy to me. I want to keep that.'

Eila pressed send. 'Done.'

On that happy note, they continued to decorate the tree creating more happy memories together.

Over the next few days other shops put their Christmas decorations up, including Kity. Tinsel and extra lights adorned her knitting shop window display and she put lights up in her shed too. The small silver tree in the shop window was decorated with knitted tree ornaments — knitted baubles, bells, a Christmas tree and knitted stars, with a sparkly yarn star on the top of the tree.

Her sock video on the shop's website proved to be popular with customers and made her feel that making knitting videos was something she'd include regularly.

A lesson at the bar restaurant's function room to practise their first dance for their wedding encouraged Kity and Lochlan to select a waltz and a romantic Scottish song. Jock had given them a selection, and they'd both loved the music.

The dance floor that Lochlan had incorporated into the new house was ideal for them to then practise it themselves.

'I could get used to dancing here at night with you,' Kity told Lochlan as they waltzed around by the warmth of the log fire and glow of the Christmas tree.

'I made it so we could use it for entertaining friends, but now I'm thinking of the other benefits.' He pulled her into a loving embrace and kissed her. Then they danced on. 'Are you all set for our trip to Edinburgh in the morning?'

Kity's eyes lit up with excitement. 'Yes, what time are we leaving?'

'Early, before eight, if that suits you.'

Kity nodded enthusiastically. 'I love Edinburgh.'

'I've had a look again at the kilt shop's website and I know what I want, so I shouldn't be too long in there, and then we can go round the city together.'

They'd decided on a couple of jewellers to try for their wedding rings after they'd arrived, so everything was organised — except the weather.

'The forecast is fine,' Lochlan assured her. 'No snow is forecast until we get back here.'

Gordon had missed going for his daily dip in the sea, so at the crack of dawn on the morning that Kity and Lochlan were due to head to Edinburgh, he braved the icy cold.

No one was around to see him wearing his swimming trunks and a towel around his shoulders. He dropped the towel on the sand and scampered into the sea, catching his breath as he took a short bracing dip.

Hurrying back out, he shook the water off his hair, threw the towel on and ran back to the tea shop to shower there.

He planned to make a start on baking rich fruit cakes and chocolate cakes for the tea shop.

With his day planned out, he got dressed and felt invigorated from his winter dip.

Firing up the ovens, he rustled up a batch of scones and rolls, and while they baked he started measuring out the flour, butter, sugar, dried fruit, chocolate and other ingredients for the cakes and prepared the large baking tins.

The warmth of the kitchen contrasted with the wintry scene outside the window. The back garden looked like it had been iced white and sprinkled with sugar crystals.

He'd lit the fire in the front shop and switched on the fairy lights, hoping customers would like the festive welcome on a cold morning.

The morning was taking its time to wake up and the cottages and farmhouses glowed with lights against the dark winter backdrop before the daylight shone a pale grey arch over the village and the coast.

Embroidery Cottage was all aglow with Christmas lights. Euan had helped Poppy put outdoor lights up on the front of the cottage and draped on the tree at the side of it.

Poppy ate her cereal in the kitchen before snuggling up cosy in the living room to get on with her embroidery work. Customers' online orders showed the popularity of her Christmas and winter patterns with thread to go with them. She drank her tea and planned to film finishing the Christmas tree she'd been embroidering in the hoop as customers were requesting to see how she satin stitched the star, baubles and added the French knots.

The wedding plans were in hand and she only had one more lesson with Euan to perfect their waltz. So that was something else she could tick–box off her list soon.

She'd completed the embroidery on her wedding dress and veil, and Kity had accepted her offer to embroider her name and Lochlan's on the hemline of her dress.

The toile for Kity's dress had now been replaced with the chiffon fabric. Judy had made short work of sewing it. And Kity had been told that the wedding dress was a gift from Judy and Jock.

A few of the bee ladies had popped in to borrow tea dresses from Judy, and take a peek at Kity's dress taking shape. And unknown to Kity, the bee members were secretly making a wedding quilt for her and Lochlan, along with items for their new house including cushions and oven mitts.

Poppy set up her camera for filming and began by showing how she used her lightbox to trace the pattern on to the white cotton fabric ready for embroidering. Then she demonstrated the techniques on the Christmas tree she'd half finished so they could see all the stitches in the pattern.

Minnie stacked the magazine rack with the new order that had arrived that morning. She loved when the Christmas editions of the magazines came out because she liked to read the features on festive decorations, things to make for gifts and recipes. The bridal magazines had already been picked up by Gordon and Lochlan and appreciated by Kity and Eila. Another bridal edition had arrived in the latest batch and she was sure it would be snapped up by them or Poppy.

Pearl came in to buy milk, eggs and a sliced loaf and caught Minnie engrossed in one of the magazine patterns.

Minnie jokingly forced herself to close the magazine and put it for sale on the rack. She indicated that she'd brought her craft bag with her. 'I'm working on a set of cushion covers for Kity and Lochlan. I should get wee bits of the appliqué hand sewn while I'm getting on with my day.'

Minnie was often to be found sitting behind her shop counter sewing something, between serving customers.

'I'm going to get on with their wedding quilt,' said Pearl, reaching down to pat Bracken. 'We made good progress with it last night at your house. I've time on my hands today to work on it. On a winter's day like this it'll be nice to sit by the fire and make their quilt.'

'The hexies seemed like a pretty idea for the quilt, and seeing it all come together last night, I really love it.'

They'd been working on a wedding quilt for Poppy and Euan, with help from other members of the bee. But now with time running short for a second wedding design, they'd used one of Minnie's favourite patchwork patterns.

'The sky blue backing fabric with a white polka dot suits the design,' said Minnie. 'I think we should use that as the binding. It'll make such a lovely edging around the quilt.'

Pearl agreed. 'I'll see if I can get the quilt ready so that all we'll need to do is hand sew the binding on.

We can do that together another night at your house or mine, and that'll be their wedding gift finished.'

With their plans settled, Pearl bought her groceries and then left Minnie to resist looking through the magazines again.

Minnie had tried to entice Bracken to go out for an early morning walk, but he was having none of it, preferring to snuggle in his basket and snooze in between receiving attention from the customers.

The day hadn't yet brightened, and the sea was deceivingly calm, rippling like watered silk beneath the pale grey sky.

Pearl was familiar with days like this, and it bolstered her plan to stay in by the fire and quilt.

Edinburgh glistened with a crisp layer of frost in the morning light. Kity and Lochlan emerged from the jewellery shop where they'd purchased their traditional wedding rings — classic gold bands.

Kity linked her arm through Lochlan's as they went for a walk in the cold, fresh air heading towards the Royal Mile.

She squeezed his arm and smiled up at him. 'The rings are perfect.'

'They are,' he agreed, keeping them safe in his jacket pocket.

Kity wore a sky blue scarf tucked into the neckline of her cream wool coat, slim–fitting dark cords and boots.

Lochlan checked the time. 'We'll go for a walk along the Old Town before I go to get my kilt.'

Meandering through the historic part of the city, they enjoyed their morning out together, peering in the shop windows and admiring the magnificent architecture that rose up into the December sky.

Soon, it was time for them to temporarily go their separate ways as Lochlan was due to buy his kilt and accessories.

'I'm planning to do some Christmas shopping while I'm here,' said Kity.

They agreed where to meet back up in Princes Street.

Waving to Lochlan as he walked away, Kity felt a rush of excitement at being in the heart of Edinburgh on a shopping trip.

She bought herself a pair of white satin wedding slippers to wear with her dress, along with new white lingerie for the occasion. Next on her shopping list were gift items and the selection available in the stores and specialist little niches enabled her to find lots of Christmas presents to take home with her.

Lochlan was impressed with the range of kilts, jackets, waistcoats and other items available in the shop. The staff welcomed him, and their suggestions for everything from the sporran to the skean dhu and socks resulted in him being expertly kitted out as a groom. He selected a tartan in shades of grey to wear with a white shirt, tie, dark jacket, waistcoat and brogues.

Leaving the shop laden with a few bags, he headed to Princes Street to meet back up with Kity. She was waiting for him, smiling hopefully when she saw all the bags he was carrying.

She held up her load of shopping bags too. 'I think we've both done well.'

'I'm not giving anything away when I say that I got a great kilt, jacket and waistcoat. They fit and don't need any alterations, so we're good to go if you want to head home. Though we could put our bags in the car and then go for something to eat.'

'Let's do that. I'm enjoying being in Edinburgh. I love living in our village by the sea, but it's nice to have a day out together in the city.'

For the remainder of the day they had lunch, explored Edinburgh, went for afternoon tea, and then as the daylight started to wane, they headed back to the car and Lochlan drove them home.

The forecast had kept its promise not to snow until they got home, and as they drove through the forest down to the shore, snowflakes began to flutter in the twilight.

Lochlan dropped Kity off at her shop. She carried her Christmas shopping inside, while he drove home to hang up his kilted groom outfit without her seeing what he intended wearing. She knew the bare minimum, mainly that he'd be kilted and kitted out in his groom's finery. Whatever he wore, Kity was confident he'd look smart for their wedding.

Wrapping paper was included in her purchases, and while the kettle boiled for a cup of tea, she started organising wrapping some of the gifts she'd bought. Labelling them, she put them under the tinsel Christmas tree she'd put up in the living room.

Then she flopped down on the sofa for the remainder of the night by the fire and made a start on knitting Lochlan's jumper.

Lochlan sent her a late night message. *I tried the whole kiltie outfit on to check that it's all sorted for the wedding. It is, so I've hung it up in the wardrobe.*

Kity replied. *I'm sure you'll look handsome. I had a great day with you in Edinburgh.*

I had a wonderful time with you. And I've got the wedding rings here safe. I tried mine on again. I can't wait to wear it for real.

Not long now.

I know. Nearly time for Poppy and Euan's big day. And then us.

Sleep tight. x

You too, Kity. x

CHAPTER FOURTEEN

The lights glowed in the windows of Euan's farmhouse. It was well past midnight, but he was steeped in things to do — including putting up a large Christmas tree to surprise Poppy. The fresh scent of the real tree filled the air as he draped the fairy lights around the branches and then added baubles and other decorations.

He always put a tree up, but this Christmas felt extra special because he was about to marry Poppy and she'd be moving into the farmhouse. His first Christmas with true love in his life. That was definitely something worth celebrating with two sets of colourful fairy lights. No one was going to miss this tree in the dark depths of the flower field, and he hoped Poppy would see it from her cottage.

Poppy had worked late on her pattern designs. Time had slipped away, and it was only when she realised that the roaring log fire was barely a glowing ember that she knew it was so late.

Tidying up, she got ready for bed, but as she turned the lights off in the living room, she saw the large Christmas tree aglow in the window of Euan's farmhouse.

Smiling to herself, she messaged him. *I love your Christmas tree.*

Euan replied. *I'm pleased you like it.*
Busy day tomorrow?

Yes, the lads are helping me to put the marquee up ready for the dress rehearsal.

It's so exciting. Poppy checked the time. *And so late at night! I'm up early in the morning.*

Euan sighed. *So am I. We'd better get some sleep.*

After agreeing with Euan and saying goodnight, Poppy checked her planner list. The dress rehearsal for the wedding was due and she reminded herself about the things she needed to prepare before going to bed.

They'd told those involved in the rehearsal, from the bridal party to others assisting with the reception, to dress casual. From the chatter around the village, almost everyone was due to attend, except Gordon. The timing of the rehearsal was set for when the shops, like Minnie's grocery, closed for the night around teatime, so that shop owners like Minnie, Kity and Eila could take part without interruption to their businesses. Euan suggested that Gordon shouldn't close the tea shop as he'd be closing it to cater for the wedding day. As best man, Gordon's duties were discussed verbally, and Euan planned to record the rehearsal so Gordon could see what went on. And Judy and Jock's staff were covering for them.

Butterflies of excitement kept Poppy awake before she eventually drifted off to sleep.

Euan fell sound asleep almost as soon as he went to bed, knowing that the plans were shaping up nicely. Parties in a marquee were a fairly regular occurrence in the village, and often his field was used for the events, so he wasn't concerned about that aspect. As for the wedding itself, he was looking forward to marrying Poppy, but as the time was approaching, even his calm nature was starting to feel the excitement build.

Lochlan stood on the porch of his house drinking a mug of tea early the next morning. The heat from the tea wafted into the cold air as he gazed out across the snow–covered fields. The snow was blue–white and he liked that the days had a tendency to match the mood of the landscape.

He planned to build a two–seater swing chair for the porch where he could sit with Kity on warmer days and long, languid evenings, unwinding after a busy day.

As he stood there gazing out at the beautiful winter scenery, he noticed activity coming from Euan's field. Lights shone in the semi–darkness and the sound of voices drifted in the calm air.

The marquee was being erected.

Lochlan downed the remainder of his tea, grabbed his tool bag and warm jacket from inside the hallway, and headed over to see if he could be of assistance. His sturdy boots crunched through the deep snow on the flower field as he approached Euan whose back was turned while he put all his strength into wrestling the marquee into shape.

'Need a hand?' Lochlan offered.

Euan glanced round at the sound of the unexpected voice and volunteer. 'Thanks, the lads are used to helping me put the marquee up, but it has its foibles.' He tugged at one of the edges of the tarpaulin, straightening it out, while the lads erected the pole structure. 'I'd welcome a builder like yourself.'

Lochlan got tore in, assisting Euan while the lads did their part.

Kity watched Lochlan in the distance working as part of the team of men putting the marquee up for the wedding.

She sat near the window of her kitchen having a bowl of porridge for breakfast. A rush of excitement went through her, realising that soon she'd be one of Poppy's bridesmaids wearing the lovely dress that Eila had now finished making. The dress rehearsal was due the following day, and then the wedding day itself for Poppy and Euan.

The time was roaring in so fast. She'd promised to attend the bee night later and was happy to have a get together with the ladies to talk about both the weddings.

The bee night members had requested a knitting night, and Kity had agreed to show them her techniques for knitting Fair Isle and other patterns using Shetland wool. She'd promised this before knowing that Lochlan was due to propose and she'd be up to her eyeballs in wedding plans. But she loved knitting and the company of like–minded members of the bee, so she was looking forward to the evening.

Watching again out her kitchen window that overlooked the flower field, her heart squeezed seeing Lochlan, so strong and capable and willing to help Euan. The kindness and fun of the local community bolstered her resolve that she'd found the perfect location to make a life with Lochlan.

Pausing for a tea break, Euan, Lochlan and the others had the whole marquee erected by the late morning.

Lochlan tested the flooring with his boots. 'Solid enough but with a bit of spring for the dancing.'

'Remember to tell Jock that,' said Euan. 'If I faff my first dance with Poppy, I'm blaming the bouncy boards.'

Lochlan laughed. 'I got the same warning from Jock when he gave Kity and me our lesson. *Don't dance like you're wearing clumpy boots*, or something along those lines.'

'You're wearing a kilt, so you should have plenty of shoogle in your step.'

'I hope so. I've been wearing my new brogues around the house to break them in, but don't tell Jock. I'll blame my brogues if I balls up my wedding waltz.'

Euan started unravelling the fairy lights that were to be draped around the marquee to create a sparkling starry sky effect. 'I'm thinking that our lassies will keep us right.'

'Especially Poppy. She can outdance Jock.'

Euan agreed. 'I hear that Kity is showing the bee members how to knit Fair Isle tonight. Poppy wants to learn to do it, so she's going along.'

'Yes, Kity mentioned that the bee is on tonight in the tea shop.'

As Euan unravelled the lights, Lochlan admired the arch that was leaning against one of the buffet tables.

'Is this your wedding arch?'

'Yes, I haven't sorted the base for it yet, but once I've got it steady, I'll wrap it in greenery and flowers.'

Lochlan took charge of the arch. 'It's got a wee wobble. I can rectify that for you.' He grabbed his tool bag.

They chatted while working.

'Are you and Kity having a wedding arch?' said Euan.

'No, we're having a small ceremony to exchange our vows in the living room of the house with a few guests present,' Lochlan explained. 'Kity's happy with this arrangement. But Dougal insists on walking into the room with her on his arm as she's going to be part of the family. And he's doubling as my best man.'

'Jock is walking Poppy down the aisle.' Euan gestured to the area leading into the marquee to the wedding arch. His best man was Gordon.

The tea shop kitchen was filled with the aroma of cakes baking while Gordon made a large pot of leek and potato soup for the daily menu. Clootie dumpling was boiling on the stove and the scent of the treacle, cinnamon and other mixed spices filtered through the air.

His selection of confectionery had been selling well, especially his new festive boxes of chocolates that included truffles, nougat, chocolate–dipped tablet and bon bons.

In the afternoon he'd rustle up tasty treats for the bee night.

The whirring of sewing machines sounded from the function room at the back of the tea shop. A few members, including Minnie and Pearl, had arrived early in the evening to finish items they were stitching, especially the quilted wedding gifts.

Minnie checked the time and hurried on with her machining. 'Kity and Poppy will be here soon,' she said to Pearl.

Increasing her productivity, Pearl whizzed through finishing off the quilted items.

They were so busy they didn't see Kity and Poppy arrive in the midst of other members.

Minnie suddenly glanced up and saw them. 'Avert your eyes!'

Pearl hurried to hide the gifts she'd been working on, and stuffed them in her craft bag.

'I didn't see anything,' Kity assured them, turning the other way.

'Neither did I,' Poppy seconded.

'Okay, you can turn around now,' Minnie announced, having tucked her quilting away.

Other members arrived in a flurry of chatter and excitement, taking off their jackets and coats and setting up the tables and chairs to enjoy an evening of knitting.

Kity had brought patterns and a selection of Shetland wool and other yarn to share. But first, she made an announcement.

'While we're all here, I wanted to say a huge thank you to Judy for making my wedding dress. She's really pulled it off so beautifully. I don't know if I've been more of a hindrance than a help, especially when I sewed part of the chiffon hem inside out.'

'It was the neatest wrong hem I've ever had to unpick,' said Judy.

The ladies laughed.

'But Judy sorted it, and now my dress is ready to wear. And thanks to Poppy for embroidering our names on the dress. This makes it so special.'

There were hugs all round.

Kity handed out copies of the pattern she intended showing them. 'I thought I'd demonstrate how to knit a Fair Isle hat on the round. I know a lot of you are experienced knitters, but it's fun to have a knitting bee night.'

The patterns were handed around, and some members had brought items they were already knitting, happy to sit and knit and chatter.

'I love the wee knitted decorations on the Christmas tree in your shop window,' Eila said to Kity.

Digging into her craft bag, Kity produced copies of the knitted star pattern, little Christmas tree, bauble and other decoration designs.

The interest in these sparked several members to start knitting the decorations.

While the knitting and gossip was exchanged, Kity began to show how she knitted the Fair Isle hat. 'This is a great way to build your skills. Remember to use a stitch marker when you cast on so you can gauge your rounds.'

Poppy sat beside Kity, watching her technique, knitting a hat on circular needles.

'I love the effect of Fair Isle knitting,' Poppy enthused.

'The colourwork is wonderful to knit,' said Kity. 'But notice that I'm only using two colours per row when I'm knitting this pattern, even though it's multi–coloured.'

Poppy and others tried their hand at the Fair Isle hat pattern, and other members with knitting experience picked up handy tips from Kity too.

Members helped and encouraged each other, and chatted about the forthcoming weddings and the dress rehearsal.

Gordon brought through tea, scones and cake and this was shared along with plenty of gossip.

'I got a message from Abby. She says that she's staying in Dublin with Josh for Christmas,' Minnie told them. 'So they won't be back for the weddings.'

'Are they still getting married in the New Year?' said Pearl.

'Yes, Abby says they'll start to plan their wedding when they get home from their trip to Dublin,' Minnie confirmed.

Pearl held up a craft bag. 'These are the last of the favours that I've made, and the quilted coasters for the reception,' she said to Poppy. 'I'll take them up to the farmhouse tomorrow.'

The bridesmaid outfits and accessories were being stored in Euan's farmhouse in two of the spare rooms. The dresses were hung in the second bedroom ready for the bridesmaids on the day of the wedding. They were all helping each other to do their hair and makeup, and two of the bee ladies were experienced in hairdressing.

The favours and bits and pieces for the reception were kept in another spare room.

Gordon brought through a plate of miniature Victoria sponge cakes. 'I was thinking of serving these for your reception,' he said to Kity. 'Anyone want to try a taste test?'

Kity was the first to lift one of the individual sponges filled with jam and cream. The other members helped themselves too.

Kity nodded, her mouth full of the tasty treat.

'I've filled some with strawberry jam and others with raspberry or bramble,' Gordon explained. 'Let me know if you have a favourite.'

'The raspberry was delicious,' Kity told him, and then selected one with bramble jam. She nodded again and mumbled. 'They're both equally tasty.'

The other ladies agreed.

'That's what I thought,' Gordon admitted. 'Maybe I'll make a mixed selection.'

'Yes please,' said Kity.

Gordon took a piece of paper from his pocket. 'I've shortlisted other cakes and confectionery. Have a look and let me know later what you think.'

'Thank you, Gordon.' Kity sipped her tea and read the cake contenders. 'I definitely want the shortbread hearts.'

Minnie, Eila, Judy and others came over to take a peek.

'Mini chocolate eclairs,' said Minnie.

'And white chocolate cake,' Eila added. 'Anything with chocolate gets my approval.'

'Oooh!' said Pearl. 'Scottish strawberry tarts.'

'Chocolate truffles,' Judy pointed out.

'I'd like those,' Kity agreed.

The ladies helped Kity select the cakes and confectionery for her afternoon tea wedding reception.

When Gordon came through to top up their tea, Kity handed him the amended list. 'These are the winners.'

Gordon skimmed the list and read those that were ticked as favourites. 'I can make these, and it's a good choice of flavours. I'll bake scones of course to go along with the cakes and make dainty sandwiches too.'

'I appreciate you doing this,' Kity told Gordon.

'It'll be fun, and I love a challenge. Besides, I want to throw in a couple of new recipes of my own,' he said.

The knitting evening finally drew to a close and the ladies packed up their craft bags, and settled their bill with Gordon.

Poppy was delighted with the start she'd made on knitting the hat and tucked it carefully into her bag. 'Thanks for showing me how to do this. I want to finish knitting it.'

'Drop by the shop if you get stuck with the pattern,' said Kity. 'And I'll show you how I cast off.'

'I'll do that.'

'Lochlan has arrived to walk you home,' Minnie told Kity, seeing him coming into the tea shop.

Kity put her coat on, said her goodnights to the ladies and Gordon, and then headed out with Lochlan.

'Did you have fun with your knitting?' he said as they walked along to the knitting shop.

'Yes, and Gordon let us sample some of the cakes he's planning for our wedding reception. I hope it was okay for me to tell him the ones we liked the most.' 'I'm happy for you to choose the cakes, Kity.'

She listed the favourites and he nodded. 'They all sound tasty.'

Cuddling close to him as they walked along, she looked out at the sea, glistening in the freezing night, and then gazed up at the stars scattered across the sky. 'The cold nights create such wonderful starry skies. If I was an artist I'd paint them.'

'You are an artist. Your knitting is a creative art. The things you knit and design are beautiful.' They'd arrived outside her shop and he gestured to her window display lit up with fairy lights.

Kity smiled and kissed him. 'Maybe I'll knit something with stars and snowflakes — a snowy winter night theme. A jumper, or a shawl so that I can wrap the feeling of these nights around myself.'

Lochlan gazed down at her and wrapped his arms around her. 'You should. To remember this special time, with the wedding so close.'

'I will.'

He kissed her. 'This is our time, Kity. You and me.'

They went inside and by the glow of the lights in the window, she put her craft bag down.

Lochlan noticed she'd been reading the new bridal magazine. It was open where she'd left it on the counter. He smiled to himself.

'Do you want a cup of tea before you go?' she offered. 'And I've tattie scones if you're interested.'

He started to take his jacket off. 'I'm interested.' He followed her upstairs.

'Could you light the fire while I make the tea,' Kity called through to him from the kitchen.

The fire was set for lighting, and he lit the kindling and watched it spark into life.

Kity grilled the tattie scones and buttered them while they were still hot.

Lochlan carried the tea through to the living room and they sat by the glow of the fire enjoying their supper and chatting.

'The marquee is all set for the dress rehearsal tomorrow,' he said. 'It's looking lovely inside. There's a bridal arch. Do you think we should have something like that?' He pictured he could make one.

Kity shook her head. 'I like our plan to get married in the house. We don't need an arch. We'll have lots of fairy lights, a Christmas tree and sparkle.'

'And candles and flowers.'

'And each other.'

Lochlan's voice deepened to a rich whisper. 'That's all I've ever wanted.'

CHAPTER FIFTEEN

Minnie's delivery of Christmas hampers arrived early in the morning. She put one out on display in the grocery shop window and the others were in her storeroom. The hampers were popular with customers and she ordered plenty every year.

She opened the lid of the gift basket and looked at the selection of luxury biscuits, traditional tins of treats such as specialist tea, chocolates, miniature bottles of whisky, jars of jam, pickles, cheese, a fruit cake, Christmas pudding, and other festive delights.

The one on display was always earmarked for Minnie's Christmas treat to herself. Later, she used the baskets and the fancy tins to store her craft items. She still had a festive design tin from years ago that she kept spools of thread in.

Euan came in, shrugging the cold morning from his broad shoulders.

'I'll take two of your large tins of fancy biscuits please, Minnie.'

She lifted them from the shelf behind her and put them on the counter while Euan loaded up on extra milk. 'For folks tea at the dress rehearsal,' he explained, paying for everything and seemingly in a rush to get back to the farmhouse.

'I hear the marquee is looking lovely,' she said, bagging his items.

'It is, thanks to everyone's efforts. I'm dealing with the flowers today, including the bouquets.' He shook the dismay from his thoughts. 'The wedding's nearly here.'

'I'll see you at the rehearsal after I close the shop today,' Minnie confirmed.

Euan nodded firmly as he grabbed the groceries. 'See you later then,' he said, and hurried back out.

Minnie had brought a change of clothes with her to the shop and planned to wear a nice dress even though she could've worn the jumper, cardigan and skirt she was wearing. According to Pearl and Judy, they were of a similar mind, so she expected that the bridesmaids would all turn up to the rehearsal looking smart.

Gordon skipped swimming in the sea even though he was up extra early. A dook in the freezing water wasn't what put him off his stride. It was not having enough hours in the day to complete all the work he needed to do. For a start, Poppy and Euan's wedding cake needed the icing finished. A task he was keen to do well. He'd worked on it the previous night, planning to add the finishing touches to it during the day, while keeping the tea shop ticking over.

The kitchen was a hive of productivity. The morning rolls were baking in one oven, while Dundee cakes baked in another. Somehow he'd found the time to make chocolate truffles and Scottish tablet. And he'd promised customers that his popular stovies would be on the daily menu.

The timers on the ovens, and alerts on his phone as extra food timers, were going off at such a rate that he found himself singing a Christmas song in time to the pings.

'Someone's very cheery this morning,' Jock said, bounding in carrying a large box of fresh farm eggs.

'At least I'm dancing to my own tune,' Gordon chirped, pretending to do a jig while he worked.

'I see dance lessons in your future,' Jock teased him.

'Only when I'm practising for my first waltz with Eila. Until then, I'll make up my own moves to my own out of rhythm steps.'

'You're not a bad dancer, Gordon. And speaking of dancing, are you and Eila going to step up after Poppy and Euan do their waltz at the wedding?'

Gordon frowned. 'Are we supposed to?'

Jock shrugged. 'Best man duties and all that.'

'Right, well, I suppose so. I'll warn Eila to watch her step when I waltz her around the marquee.' Then he looked at the large box of eggs Jock was holding.

'The farmer delivered extra this morning, so I thought with all the baking you're doing, you could use them.'

'That's very thoughtful, Jock. They'll be so handy.'

'I'll put them over here on the table. And Euan says he's going to record the rehearsal.'

'Yes, I need to keep the tea shop open tonight. It's been busy lately. Euan says my best man duties aren't too fussy, so I'll do my utmost on the day.'

'I'm popping up to the marquee with Judy. But on the wedding day, I'll be swinging between being a guest and keeping the buffet going. A bit like yourself. Best man and best caterer.'

'Between the two of us, we'll make the buffet special,' said Gordon.

Jock rubbed his hands together. 'I'm looking forward to it. I do like a wedding — and a dance.'

Gordon continued to ice Poppy and Euan's wedding cake, adding pink and white fondant roses to the three tiers that were covered with white royal icing.

'That's a winter wedding masterpiece,' said Jock, admiring the cake.

'Thanks, I'll have it finished soon.'

'I'm sure that Poppy and Euan will be delighted with it.' Leaving Gordon to get on with his day, Jock headed away.

He met Eila on her way in carrying one of the hampers. 'Morning, Jock.'

'Ah, I see Minnie's hampers have arrived. It's not Christmas until we've all got one. I have ours on order. Folk snap them up.'

'I did.' Eila had bought it on impulse. 'I thought I'd share it with Gordon.'

'He's up to his eyes in icing cakes, so I think he'll appreciate a wee treat.'

Eila headed through to the kitchen carrying the hamper. 'I bought this from Minnie. I'll put it upstairs so we can share it. The hamper is filled with tasty treats, but can I have the hamper when we've scoffed everything?'

'Yes, and thanks for buying it. I love a Christmas hamper.'

'Minnie says she uses the empty hampers and biscuit and sweetie tins to store her sewing and craft items. I fancy doing that too.' Delighted with her purchase, she carried it upstairs, while Gordon got on with his work.

Gordon was so busy cooking and baking that his day flew in. But he'd managed to keep his customers happy with the stovies, Scotch broth, scones and a variety of cakes, while racking and stacking items he was making in advance for the wedding reception.

His lists had lists, but somehow he'd ticked off more than he'd added to, so by the time Euan called him in the early evening, he was ready to take in what was happening at the dress rehearsal.

Propping his phone up against a baking bowl, he watched and listened to Euan, while continuing to make the pink iced fairy cakes for the bridal buffet.

Euan's smile was tense. 'Everything is fine. Jock has suggested that the buffet tables be extended to the bar area. I agree, so Lochlan's away in his van to pick up the extra tables from one of the farmers.'

Gordon viewed the mild chaos in the background behind Euan, but kept his thoughts on the melee to himself. 'It's better to have more tables so that we can present the buffet food nicely.'

'Yes, so that's in hand. And over here is where you'll stand as my best man while I exchange vows with Poppy. The ceremony itself is sort of short and sweet. Then while we're having our photos taken under the wedding arch, the chairs will be folded away and the floor cleared quickly for the dancing.'

A local photographer had been hired to take the wedding photos, but guests had been encouraged to film and snap pictures too. Poppy wanted lots of pictures and video footage of the wedding and reception.

'Will I need to give a speech?' said Gordon.

'It's not a lavish affair or a sit down meal, so just say a few words as we drink the first toast of the evening. Jock's going to give a brief speech too, and then we'll enjoy the dancing.'

Gordon peered at the screen. 'Is that Eila over there beside the other bridesmaids?'

Euan glanced round. 'Yes.' He beckoned to Eila. 'I've got Gordon on the phone. Come and give him a wave.'

Eila hurried over, bringing Kity and Judy with her. Her lovely face smiled at him. 'We're having great fun practising being bridesmaids. Isn't that right?'

Kity and Judy chipped in, agreeing, giggling and held up what appeared to be glasses of whisky.

'Jock made lemonade cocktails for us,' Eila explained.

Gordon laughed, seeing the rosy glow on Eila's cheeks. 'Jock's cocktails have a real kick in them.'

Eila frowned and held up her half empty glass. 'I downed the first one like it was a lemonade shandy. But I think there's a wee tipple of the strong stuff in this brew. I'm feeling quite...lively.'

Euan encouraged the bridesmaids to wave to Gordon and then get back to the rehearsal with Poppy.

Gordon laughed. 'If this is how lively the rehearsal is, I'm betting the actual wedding is going to be...extra special.'

'Tactfully put,' said Euan. 'Poppy's dragged me on to the dance floor three times to practise our waltz. Jock's playing plenty of music to get people into the party mood, so the floor's been well–checked.'

'Euan!' Lochlan called from the doorway of the marquee. 'Where do you want the tables?'

'Over there,' said Euan, and then spoke to Gordon. 'I'll phone you back.' And he was gone.

Gordon smiled to himself, picturing the friendly fiasco up in the flower field.

Jock phoned a few minutes later, his face peering cheerily at Gordon. 'Was it you or me that promised to make tipsy laird trifle for the buffet?'

'You told me that Poppy wanted a Scottish trifle and you said you'd make it for her wedding buffet. I'm making the chocolate Yule log and the Edinburgh fog.' The latter was a Scottish dessert made with a mix of ingredients including double cream, crushed macaroon biscuits, almonds and whisky.

'Okay, and I'm making plenty of sandwiches,' Jock added, and then he was gone too, pulled into the friendly fray that was rumbling in the background.

Snow had fallen overnight, then stopped in the morning, gifting Poppy and Euan a winter wonderland for their wedding day. The sun pretended it was summer and blinked through the haze, like a bridal veil draped over the trees, rising up from the forest. The air was still, as if holding its breath in readiness for the festivities.

The shimmer from the sea highlighted the marquee in all its bridal beauty. Adorned with lights, inside and out, it glittered, sprinkled with snow crystals.

Squeals of delight resonated through Euan's bustling farmhouse, filled with the bridesmaids getting dressed, but separate from the groom's guests including the best man.

The snow bride looked in the wardrobe mirror, seeing herself as she'd long dreamed she'd be, wearing the beautiful wedding dress encrusted with crystals and a veil trailing like a princess.

Poppy wore her hair down, while Kity, Eila, Judy, Minnie and Pearl, wore theirs pinned up with diamante clasps. A small, glittering, princess–style tiara held Poppy's veil secure.

The oyster pink dresses of the bridesmaids were gorgeous and worn with the knitted pink boleros.

Judy fussed with Poppy's dress, while the ladies bolstered her confidence. Butterflies of excitement made Poppy clasp tightly to the bouquet Euan had made for her. All their bouquets were created from the fresh greenery in the flower fields and secured with ribbons.

White winter flowers including jasmine, jingle bells clematis and winter's snowman camellia were coupled with greenery.

Poppy's bouquet had white ribbons, while pink ribbons trailed from the bridesmaids' flowers.

Minnie smiled at Poppy and gave her hands a reassuring squeeze. 'You look beautiful.'

The others chimed–in with equal praise.

'Thank you,' said Poppy. She heard her own nervousness in her voice and took a deep, steadying breath.

'Are you ready?' Judy said to Poppy, while Pearl and Minnie checked that Kity and Eila were all set to head to the marquee. A path had been cleared and a carpet rolled out so they could walk the short distance from the farmhouse to the marquee.

Poppy took a final look at herself in the mirror. 'Yes.'

The groom was standing under the floral arch in the marquee, backed by his best man, Gordon. Other men supporting the groom, including Lochlan, stood in readiness too.

At the doorway of the marquee, Jock, wearing his finest kilted attire, smiled at Poppy and offered her his arm to walk her down the aisle.

Judy fussed with Poppy's veil, so it would trail behind her as she walked down towards Euan at the bridal arch.

Music played, announcing that the bride had arrived, and all heads turned to watch Poppy, a vision in white satin and crystals walk down to Euan.

The groom's reaction showed he was taken aback by her beauty. He'd expected Poppy to shine like the winter sunlight, but nothing could've prepared him for how wonderful she looked. He thought his heart would burst as Jock placed her beside him and then stepped back to take his position along with Gordon and Lochlan.

As Poppy and Euan exchanged their loving vows, Kity saw Lochlan glance at her as if to say...he couldn't wait for their wedding day too.

As the newly married couple kissed under the arch, and then turned to face their guests, cheers and applause filled the marquee.

While photographs were taken as planned, Jock helped organise the chairs to be tucked away quickly to clear the dance floor. One of his staff from the bar restaurant manned the makeshift bar, and Jock was on hand along with Judy to help serve the drinks if needed.

Before the celebrations started, Gordon tinged his glass of champagne ready to give a short speech as best man before the dancing began.

A hush fell over the guests as they eagerly awaited Gordon's speech. He'd never done this before, but while he'd been baking cakes galore at the tea shop, he'd had time to think what he wanted to say.

'I was going to make light–hearted comments about Euan falling so hard for Poppy that he inveigled me into teaching him how to bake a cake to impress her,' Gordon began. 'I tried to disguise him in a chef's hat in my kitchen on a bee night, but Judy was wise to that ruse.'

Judy and the bee ladies nodded, remembering this.

Gordon smiled. 'We all know there are a few men here that have tried to impress their ladies with foolhardy dips in the freezing cold sea when it's snowing — and learning to waltz despite having no aptitude for dancing.'

The guests glanced at Lochlan, Jock and Euan, and smiled knowingly.

'But then I thought...what do I really want to tell them?' Gordon continued. 'And I decided that I wanted to say something else entirely.'

All eyes and interest were on Gordon, wondering what he'd now decided to say.

'So to Poppy and Euan, I'll say this,' said Gordon. 'While we've all been busy getting ready for the wedding, I've heard nothing but kindness and generosity from the people of this community. On the bee nights while I was in the kitchen, I could hear the ladies chatting excitedly about helping Poppy with her dress, the favours and the gifts. And then when Kity and Lochlan announced their engagement and a second wedding, the kindness and generosity didn't waver. In fact, it increased. And it made me realise that what I really want to say to Poppy and Euan is — I wish them a long and happy marriage with the joy of Christmas for the years to come — and all the love and enduring friendship from the folk in our wee community.'

Gordon raised his glass and everyone cheered and drank a toast to Poppy and Euan.

'Let the dancing begin,' Jock announced, feeling there was nothing to add to Gordon's heartfelt sentiments.

The main lights dimmed to a romantic glow as Euan escorted his new bride on to the dance floor.

Their song played, and under the fairy lights, like a starry sky, they danced together, with Euan competently leading Poppy in their wedding waltz as everyone looked on.

Euan smiled down at Poppy. 'You look beautiful,' he murmured.

'I'm so happy, Euan,' she told him.

After a couple of minutes, Gordon and Eila joined them on the floor, waltzing around. Jock and Judy then took to the floor, followed by Kity and Lochlan, Minnie and Shawn, and Dougal and Pearl. All the bridesmaids and their partners danced around the edges of the floor with Poppy and Euan in the middle. The pale pink satin dresses teamed with the soft boleros were the perfect choice for the bridesmaids' outfits, and the photographer snapped pictures of them dancing and video footage too.

The music changed seamlessly to another romantic waltz, and soon the other guests joined in the dancing.

The buffet was set up along one side of the marquee, and a couple of catering staff had been hired to help serve the guests if required.

Poppy and Euan cut their wedding cake, thanking Gordon for making the masterpiece. Gordon then expertly cut it into portions for the guests.

The Edinburgh fog and tipsy laird trifle were so popular that both were the first to disappear from the buffet.

'Would you like to get something to eat?' Euan said to Poppy.

'Yes, I've been so excited I hardly had anything all day,' Poppy told him.

Serving her up a plate of dainty sandwiches and a salad garnish, Euan joined her in enjoying the delicious delicacies and traditional favourites.

While topping up Kity's tea and getting her a slice of wedding cake from the buffet, Lochlan spoke briefly to Dougal out of earshot of Kity.

'Do you still have that lovely spare wood in your shed?' Lochlan said to Dougal.

'I do, what do you need it for?'

'I want to build a swing chair for two on the house porch.' Lochlan explained what he was planning to make.

'Nah! You don't want to build one of those.' Dougal frowned and shook his head.

Lochlan was taken aback. He'd thought that his uncle would've approved of his idea.

'Buy a couple of nice comfy outdoor chairs,' Dougal advised him.

Taking Dougal's suggestion to heart, Lochlan shelved his plans to make a love seat swing, and took Kity's tea and cake over to her.

The favours were a success, with guests loving the flower seeds in some of the bags, and the embroidery gifts in others, along with the sweet treats.

Euan and Poppy spent quite a bit of time on the dance floor. She loved wearing her bridal dress and wanted to enjoy waltzing with her new husband. Even as the music became lively, encouraging guests to join hands in circles and swirl around in ceilidh reels, Poppy and Euan barely let go of each other.

Gordon flitted between dancing with Eila, and making sure the buffet was topped up.

223

Jock helped out at the bar when it was busy, while Judy and the other bridesmaids chatted about the wedding and what a wonderful time they were having.

The reception ended late in the night with two romantic slow dances, and only the twinkling of the fairy lights.

The crystals and sequins sparkled on Poppy's dress as she danced the final slow waltz of the evening with Euan.

When it was time for the new couple to be the first to leave, Poppy threw her bouquet into the air.

Eila squealed with delight when she caught it. Gordon smiled and gave her a loving kiss.

Leaving to start their new life together, Euan and Poppy headed out into the night. As they hurried towards the farmhouse, that was ready for them with the fire lit and the Christmas tree glowing like a beacon, Euan lifted his new bride up in his arms and carried her the rest of the way and into the warmth of the farmhouse.

Guests started to filter out, heading home after one of the happiest weddings the village had enjoyed in a long time.

'We'll clear up in the morning,' Jock said to Gordon. 'Not that there's anything left from the buffet.'

'I'll pop over in the morning and give you a hand to return the tables and dismantle the marquee,' Lochlan offered.

Agreeing they'd tackle the tasks early the next day, they were the last to leave.

Jock glanced back one last time into the marquee, then turned the fairy lights off, and headed home with Judy.

Euan set Poppy down near the Christmas tree, but kept his arms around her. This was the first time they'd been alone as husband and wife, and he wanted to remember these moments and make the most of this special night.

'I had the most wonderful wedding I could ever have hoped for, Euan. I loved being a snow bride.'

He kissed her with all the love in his heart. 'I promise you that this is the type of happiness I want us to share. Even when we're busy with work or anything else. We'll always make time for each other.'

'I'll hold you to that promise,' she said, gazing up at him. He looked so handsome in his suit, with a buttonhole of white florals and greenery made from his own fields. This was the life she wanted in the Scottish village by the sea, with a wonderful man like Euan.

CHAPTER SIXTEEN

The days following Poppy and Euan's wedding were less than calm, as the village prepared to enjoy the second wedding before Christmas.

Kity sat in her knitting shop, working on the jumper she was making for Lochlan. A notepad was on the counter beside her, and in between knitting, gazing out at the sea and snowy day, she jotted down the pattern design for the stars and snowflakes shawl she planned to knit.

But as she sat in the cosy quietude of the shop, happily knitting away, having packed the orders, the last delivery going out until after Christmas, she felt that she should be busy getting ready for her wedding. And yet...everything was in hand.

Her wedding dress was finished and hanging in the spare bedroom of the new house where Lochlan had promised not to peek. Seeing how efficient it was for Poppy and Euan and their bridal party to get ready in the farmhouse, Kity and Lochlan had decided that their plan to have everything ready in the new house would work well for them too.

Poppy and Euan were enjoying a home honeymoon, but Poppy was still keen to be one of Kity's bridesmaids. Judy had helped organise tea dresses with traditional floral prints for all five bridesmaids, and these were hanging up beside Kity's wedding dress. Euan had insisted on making the bouquets and buttonholes.

Lochlan's kilted outfit hung in the main bedroom. Dougal planned to wear his kilt as best man, and other men were wearing kilts or suits.

The small, intimate wedding was all set. After the ceremony, there was the reception in the tea shop, followed by an evening of dancing in the bar restaurant. As Gordon and Jock were in charge of the latter two, Lochlan only had to make sure the fairy lights in the living room where they were holding the ceremony were draped around the bridal area where they planned to exchange their vows.

Lochlan had the lights pinned up. And two spare sets if needed.

The photographer from the previous wedding was booked, so all the main arrangements were done.

Wedding gifts from the bee ladies and others in the community were wrapped and sitting under the Christmas tree. Kity surmised that the presents included a wedding quilt for their bed and other quilted items for the house.

A phone call from Lochlan jarred Kity from her thoughts.

'Another wedding gift has just been delivered to the house. It's from Dougal.'

'What is it?'

'I was going to make a swing seat for us,' Lochlan confessed. 'But Dougal has made one as a wedding gift. It's for the porch.' He snapped a picture of it and sent it to her.

'It's perfect,' said Kity.

Lochlan told her about talking to Dougal at the wedding reception party and being dissuaded from making a seat because he was going to be gifted one.

'I thought we'd keep it wrapped until after the wedding,' Lochlan suggested.

A wave of excitement charged through Kity, realising that they were about to get married the following day.

Lochlan sensed the hesitation in Kity. 'Are you okay?'

'Yes, just feeling the jitters, in an exciting way.'

'I'm going to try and get an early night after I have my dinner,' said Lochlan.

'I have to take the orders to the post office, and then I'm locking the shop, making dinner and relaxing with my knitting before going to bed.'

Lochlan took a deep breath. 'I'll see you tomorrow, Kity. I really can't wait until we're married.'

'I feel the same.'

Ending their call on a loving note, Kity put her coat on, picked up the parcels and headed along to the post office. Snow had fallen lightly for most of the day, icing the village in a fresh layer of wintry beauty.

After dropping off the parcels, she meandered back to the knitting shop, breathing in the fresh sea air and gazing out at the lights along the coast blinking into life as the day gave way to the early twilight.

Locking up the shop, she headed upstairs to cook dinner, popping an easy to prepare pie topped with mashed potatoes into the oven. While it heated, she lit the fire in the living room and changed into her comfy pyjamas and slippers.

She'd brought her knitting from downstairs and sat it on the table in front of the fire. Knitting Lochlan's jumper would help her unwind.

Eating dinner in the kitchen, she peered out the window at the cottages and farmhouses dotted around in the snow. Lights shone from the windows and she could see the Christmas trees aglow. In the distance, across the fields, Lochlan's house was lit with fairy lights, and she pictured him having everything ready for the wedding.

After dinner, she sat in front of the fire knitting the jumper and thinking of the wonderful day ahead.

Gordon worked late at the tea shop after closing for the evening. Eila was having an early night, ready for the wedding.

Kity and Lochlan's wedding cake was finished and set aside in the kitchen. The two–tier cake looked lovely iced white. The Victoria sponge cakes were made, and the shortbread hearts, chocolate eclairs and strawberry tarts. Now all he had to make were the truffles and the white chocolate cake.

Gordon wasn't going to the wedding ceremony as he needed to have everything ready for the guests arriving for the late afternoon reception at the tea shop.

The premises would close to customers in the afternoon and reopen in the evening, but Gordon did plan to attend the wedding party in the bar restaurant later in the night.

Working away in his kitchen, he baked the cake and truffles. Then he added a few little extras to the reception menu including his new recipe fruit cake.

The warmth of the tea shop contrasted with the cold snowy night outside. Snow was forecast for the wedding day, but he pictured this would add to the Christmassy feeling of the event.

The bar restaurant was busy. Judy and Jock chatted about the wedding plans while they served customers at the bar.

'The bridesmaids are wearing tea dresses,' Judy reminded him, 'but Euan has insisted on making all our bouquets and buttonholes for the men. So remember to take a pin with you to secure your buttonhole to your jacket.'

'I will,' Jock confirmed. He planned to wear his dress kilt, jacket and accessories.

'Poppy phoned me to say that the bouquets are gorgeous. Euan has included white winter flowers, with white heather and thistles. Kity mentioned that she'd like a Scottish winter theme.'

'That sounds lovely,' said Jock.

'Euan's used white and tartan ribbons too,' Judy added.

Jock mixed a whisky cocktail while Judy poured a beer.

'I've seen Gordon's afternoon tea menu for the wedding reception,' Jock told Judy. 'It's great. But I was thinking that maybe I'd make broth or stew for the party night. The guests will have been plied with tasty cakes, scones and dainty sandwiches, but after a few dances they would enjoy a savoury supper.'

'Make your broth and stew. Customers like both.'

Jock nodded and poured glasses of wine. 'I've music lined up to keep things lively with a few romantic tunes thrown in.'

Judy nudged him. 'Always the romantic.'

Jock smiled and leaned over and gave Judy a kiss.

A party night was being held in the function room. It was one of the festive evenings they'd scheduled for the customers.

Above the music and chatter, Jock and Judy continued to make their plans for the second wedding.

The fire was nearly out by the time Kity put her knitting away. It was late at night, and as she peered out the bedroom window at the snow falling, she felt the quietude of the village. No sounds from the bar restaurant that was now closed. She surmised that she was probably the only one still up. The bride.

She smiled to herself and then climbed into bed. Snuggling under the covers, she watched the snow drift by the window.

Kity thought about Lochlan, and her wedding day, before falling asleep.

Judy and the other four bridesmaids were all wearing their tea dresses and helping each other get ready for the wedding ceremony that was being held downstairs in the living room of the new house. Their chatter and laughter added to the excitement of the day.

They were ensconced in the spare bedroom, along with Kity.

'This house is wonderful,' said Minnie.

Kity had given them a tour of the new house before they started getting ready for the wedding ceremony.

'I love the kitchen,' Pearl added.

Minnie nodded. 'It's so spacious and yet it feels homely. The traditional dressers are lovely.'

'Lochlan made them himself,' Kity told them. 'He's put so much work into the house.'

'Made with love,' said Eila. 'It's obvious that Lochlan built this with you in mind.'

Kity blushed.

'Was that a swing chair wrapped up on the porch?' Poppy said to Kity.

'Yes, it's a wedding gift from Dougal.'

'What a romantic idea, a porch swing for two,' Poppy remarked.

'I love the living room,' said Judy. 'Those large windows create a feeling of being in the heart of the countryside but with a view of the sea.'

'And the balcony off the master bedroom,' Minnie added. 'You can sit outside and gaze at the sea and across the fields.'

'It's one of the loveliest houses I've seen,' Kity told them. 'It's handy too because I can walk to my knitting shop in minutes.'

'Is that your knitting shop closed for the holidays now?' said Pearl.

'Yes, until after Christmas,' Kity explained. 'We're having a Christmas honeymoon at home, as you know. But the shop was busy yesterday with customers buying last minute yarn and patterns.'

'I'm closing my dress shop tomorrow,' Eila announced. 'Gordon has the tea shop open until Christmas Eve, but then we're having a cosy Christmas together.'

'I close my grocery shop a bit early on Christmas Eve,' Minnie explained. 'I open again after Boxing Day.'

'Jock and I keep the bar restaurant open right through Christmas,' said Judy. 'But we both love the party season, so it suits us.'

'After tomorrow, Euan and I are battening the hatches on the farmhouse,' Poppy told them, sounding delighted. 'We're going to watch festive films and have a cosy honeymoon Christmas.'

'I usually cook Christmas dinner at my house,' said Minnie. 'This year, Shawn and I have accepted an invitation to have it with Pearl and Dougal at the bar restaurant.'

'You'll all have a great time,' Judy promised. 'Jock's Christmas dinners are always popular.'

Kity gazed out the window. It had been snowing all day and the white glow reflected into the house, creating a beautiful atmosphere. 'I'm looking forward to a snowy Christmas here with Lochlan. I bought one of Minnie's hampers and so did he, so we've got plenty of festive treats to enjoy as well as cooking dinner together.'

Judy assisted Kity with her bridal veil that was pinned with diamante clasps. Lighter and shorter than

Poppy's design, it suited the style of Kity's chiffon dress.

Kity's hair was brushed smooth and fell around her shoulders, while the bridesmaids wore their hair pinned up. Her makeup was soft and subtle.

'I love this dress,' Kity said, lifting the top layer of chiffon on the skirt to let it waft down. 'Snow or not, I'm wearing it to the tea shop and to the party night at the bar restaurant.'

'You should,' Minnie told her. 'Lochlan can carry his new bride over the threshold tonight.'

Excitement swept through Kity, and she pictured Lochlan walking with her in his arms across the snow–covered field to the house late that night.

'I've brought the bouquets,' Euan called to them from along the upstairs hallway, careful not to intrude on them getting ready.

Judy and Minnie took charge of them, bringing them into the bridal hub.

'Oh, these bouquets are lovely,' Minnie enthused.

Kity lifted her bouquet and breathed in the fresh scent. 'Euan's added white heather and thistles along with the other white flowers.'

'He wanted to create the Scottish winter theme you'd mentioned,' Poppy explained.

Kity let her fingers trail along the tartan and white satin ribbons that secured the bouquet. 'It's gorgeous.'

The bridesmaids loved their bouquets too.

'They suit the tea dresses we're wearing,' said Pearl.

'They certainly do,' Eila agreed. 'There's a vintage vibe to them.'

The tea dresses blended rather than matched. The floral prints were pretty pastels, and the dresses had cap sleeves or three quarter lengths. Later, these would be worn with cardigans of varying tones from pale lemon to sky blue. The bridesmaids shared cardigans so the colours suited each dress. And Kity had a white cardigan to wear over her wedding dress when they went to the tea shop.

'Euan has made buttonholes along the same theme,' Poppy added.

'Are you ladies all set?' Jock called to them without peering in.

'Yes,' Judy replied. She waited until Jock had gone, then led the way downstairs, followed by Kity and the other bridesmaids.

A kilted Dougal was waiting on his own in the hall while the guests and groom were assembled in the living room.

Smiling at Dougal, Kity linked her arm through his.

Jock started the soft, romantic music as the bride was escorted into the living room, followed by her bridesmaids.

The glow of the fairy lights and the Christmas tree created a wonderful atmosphere for the short but romantic ceremony.

Lochlan stood looking tall and handsome in his fine kilted outfit, smiling at Kity as she walked towards him.

He wore a white shirt and tie, waistcoat, cropped dark jacket, kilt with a silver chain sporran, brogues and tartan flashes tucked into the cuffs of his long, cream socks, along with a silver skean dhu.

Kity looked beautiful in her white chiffon dress, smiling happily at Lochlan.

Dougal stepped back into the role of best man, while the loving couple exchanged their vows.

Snow fell outside the windows of the living room, giving a feeling of a true winter wonderland.

The photographer captured these moments on video and in pictures, including the special moments when the rings were exchanged, the couples first kiss and the smiles of the happy couple.

Drinks were set up beside the Christmas tree for the guests to drink a toast before heading to the tea shop.

Gordon had the fire lit in the front of the tea shop, and had adorned the function room with fairy lights. The snow scene outside in the back garden added a glow to the setting through the patio doors.

Tables and chairs were set for the guests, with the wedding cake on display.

Silver cake stands filled with cakes, scones and sandwiches sat on each table, along with lovely vintage style plates, tea cups and saucers. Candles in glass holders, some clear, some pink, were lit in readiness.

Eila had messaged Gordon that they were all on their way and that the wedding ceremony was perfect.

Hurrying through to the kitchen, Gordon changed out of his apron and put a dress waistcoat on over his white shirt for his role as chef and guest.

Everything from the tea to the festive hot chocolate was brewing nicely. A chocolate log, brandy butter and scoops of lemon sorbet and vanilla ice cream awaited the guests as added extras, along with whipped cream and sprinkles galore.

A flurry of snowflakes wafted in with the guests and the bride and groom. The chatter and laughter raised the bar of the warm atmosphere of the tea shop.

'This is your table,' Gordon said to Kity and Lochlan, gesturing to the table with a backdrop of the snow scene. 'Everyone else take a seat where you please.'

Coats, jackets and cardigans were hung up, and the chatter continued as they all seated themselves at the tables.

More photographs were taken, with Gordon standing beside Kity and Lochlan, along with best man, Dougal, and the bridesmaids.

Lochlan stood up to give a short speech at the opening champagne toast. 'Kity and I planned a small wedding before Christmas, taking many of you aback by our whirlwind engagement. We never imagined that all our friends and loved ones would help us arrange the wedding of our dreams.' He glanced at Kity to include her as planned. 'So we'd like to thank you for this wonderful gift, of a wedding we will treasure for ever.'

A resounding cheer filled the tea shop.

Standing up, Kity and Lochlan cut their classic wedding cake, and then Gordon deftly sliced it and served up pieces to all the guests.

Setting their glasses down, the guests tucked into the delicious afternoon tea.

Gordon busied himself serving up the chocolate log, extra whipped cream, ice cream and plenty of tea.

Kity ate one of the dainty fresh cress and cheese sandwiches, feeling her wedding nerves settle as she sat with Lochlan and the guests having enjoyed her dream wedding.

'Breakfast was a blur,' Lochlan said to her, helping himself to the tasty selection on the cake stand.

Laughter and joy raised the level of the afternoon tea, making it one of the most successful celebrations Gordon had held at the tea shop.

'I'm slipping out to check that everything is set for the party,' Jock whispered to Judy as the afternoon tea drew to a close.

Judy nodded. 'I'll start organising everyone to get ready to pop next door.'

Jock hurried away. It was snowing and the brisk sea breeze whipped up from the coast. The bar restaurant was busy, but a notice was pinned up stating that a private wedding reception party was being held in the function room.

Having set up the function room and music earlier in the day before attending the wedding ceremony, Jock turned the lights on and made sure that everything was ready for the guests arriving.

He'd added bridal balloons to the decor and extra Christmas lights to create a welcoming atmosphere. As he sometimes did for special functions, he'd set up a small balloon drop above the dance floor.

Judy led Kity and Lochlan and the guests from the tea shop into the bar restaurant. She'd told them to put their cardigans and coats on because it was snowing.

Kity draped her white cardigan around her shoulders and made a dash through the snow, feeling her wedding slippers brush against the icy flakes. Lochlan shielded her from the worst of the cold.

Scurrying next door, the wedding party went through to the function room and put their coats in the cloak room. Gordon stayed in the tea shop to reopen to customers for a short time, and planned to join them later.

Jock played a cheery Christmas song to get the party going, and a few voices joined in the chorus.

Lochlan pulled Kity into his arms by the glow of the Christmas lights, telling her again how beautiful she looked in her wedding dress.

She held up the hemline. 'Poppy embroidered our names. I'm keeping this for ever.'

'I'm keeping you for ever, Kity,' Lochlan said, gazing down at the one true love of his life. He kissed her lovingly, deeply and she knew in her heart that they would always be together. They'd been made for each other all along.

'Would the happy couple take to the dance floor for their first waltz?' said Jock. He'd changed the music to a song they'd told him they both enjoyed.

Clasping Kity's hand, Lochlan led her to the centre of the floor and they began to waltz while their guests smiled on.

They were soon joined by Dougal and Pearl, Poppy and Euan, and Minnie and Shawn.

While the bride and groom, the bridesmaids and their partners waltzed around, Jock released the wedding balloons he'd set up above the dance floor.

As the balloons fell down, the guests laughed and danced, enjoying the fun and festivities of another wonderful Christmas wedding.

A tasty supper of broth, stew and Christmas pudding was served later during the party.

Gordon had arrived and was dancing with Eila.

And then it was time for Kity to throw her wedding bouquet.

Minnie caught it and smiled, while everyone clapped and cheered.

At the end of the night, Lochlan wrapped Kity up in his jacket and after saying goodnight to the guests, he insisted on carrying her across the snow–covered field towards their new house.

She laughed as he walked through the snow in his brogues and thick socks, wearing his kilt.

Strong and capable, he carried her with ease, and she wrapped her arms around his shoulders, loving that it was snowing.

Kity blinked as she gazed up at the snow fluttering down from the night sky. She couldn't see the stars for the snowflakes, but she knew they were there.

'It's snowing! On our wedding day!' She looked at the flakes falling down all around them. She breathed in the fresh, night air, feeling the sense of Christmastime as they approached the house. Lights shone from the windows, and fairy lights sparkled like stars outside the house, creating a perfect welcome home.

'I've dreamed of this day for years, Kity. I've always loved you and I always will.'

'I love you too, Lochlan.'

He kissed her and she snuggled into him as he carried her over the threshold into the warmth of the house, and they looked forward to their new life together and a happy Christmas.

End

About the Author:

De-ann Black is a bestselling author, scriptwriter and former newspaper journalist. She has over 100 books published. Romance, thrillers, espionage novels, action adventure. And children's books (non-fiction rocket science books and children's fiction). She became an Amazon All-Star author in 2014 and 2015.

She previously worked as a full-time newspaper journalist for several years. She had her own weekly columns in the press. This included being a motoring correspondent where she got to test drive cars every week for the press for three years.

Before being asked to work for the press, De-ann worked in magazine editorial writing everything from fashion features to social news. She was the marketing editor of a glossy magazine.

She is also a professional artist and illustrator. Embroidery design, fabric design, dressmaking, sewing, knitting and fashion are part of her work.

Additionally, De-ann has always been interested in fitness, and was a fitness and bodybuilding champion, 100 metre runner and mountaineer. As a former N.A.B.B.A. Miss Scotland, she had a weekly fitness show on the radio that ran for over three years.

De-ann trained in Shukokai karate, boxing, kickboxing, Dayan Qigong and Jiu Jitsu. She is currently based in Scotland.

Her 16 colouring books are available in paperback, including her latest Summer Nature Colouring Book and Flower Nature Colouring Book.

Her latest embroidery pattern books include: Floral Garden Embroidery Patterns, Christmas & Winter Embroidery Patterns, Floral Spring Embroidery Patterns and Sea Theme Embroidery Patterns.

Website: Find out more at: www.de-annblack.com

Fabric, Wallpaper & Home Decor Collections:
De-ann's fabric designs and wallpaper collections, and home decor items, including her popular Scottish Garden Thistles patterns, are available from Spoonflower.
www.de-annblack.com/spoonflower

Also by De-ann Black (Romance, Action/Thrillers & Children's books). See her Amazon Author page or website for further details about her books, screenplays, illustrations, art, fabric designs and embroidery patterns.

Amazon Author page:
www.De-annBlack.com/Amazon

Romance books:

The Cure for Love Romance series:
1. The Cure for Love
2. The Cure for Love at Christmas

Scottish Highlands & Island Romance series:
1. Scottish Island Knitting Bee
2. Scottish Island Fairytale Castle
3. Vintage Dress Shop on the Island
4. Fairytale Christmas on the Island

Scottish Loch Romance series:
1. Sewing & Mending Cottage
2. Scottish Loch Summer Romance

Quilting Bee & Tea Shop series:
1. The Quilting Bee
2. The Tea Shop by the Sea
3. Embroidery Cottage
4. Knitting Shop by the Sea
5. Christmas Weddings

Sewing, Crafts & Quilting series:
1. The Sewing Bee
2. The Sewing Shop
3. Knitting Cottage (Scottish Highland romance)
4. Scottish Highlands Christmas Wedding
(Embroidery, Knitting, Dressmaking & Textile Art)

Cottages, Cakes & Crafts series:
1. The Flower Hunter's Cottage
2. The Sewing Bee by the Sea
3. The Beemaster's Cottage
4. The Chocolatier's Cottage
5. The Bookshop by the Seaside
6. The Dressmaker's Cottage

Scottish Chateau, Colouring & Crafts series:
1. Christmas Cake Chateau
2. Colouring Book Cottage

Snow Bells Haven series:
1. Snow Bells Christmas
2. Snow Bells Wedding

Summer Sewing Bee

Sewing, Knitting & Baking series:
1. The Tea Shop
2. The Sewing Bee & Afternoon Tea
3. The Christmas Knitting Bee
4. Champagne Chic Lemonade Money
5. The Vintage Sewing & Knitting Bee

The Tea Shop & Tearoom series:
1. The Christmas Tea Shop & Bakery
2. The Christmas Chocolatier
3. The Chocolate Cake Shop in New York at Christmas
4. The Bakery by the Seaside
5. Shed in the City

Tea Dress Shop series:
1. The Tea Dress Shop At Christmas
2. The Fairytale Tea Dress Shop In Edinburgh
3. The Vintage Tea Dress Shop In Summer

Christmas Romance series:
1. Christmas Romance in Paris
2. Christmas Romance in Scotland

Oops! I'm the Paparazzi series:
1. Oops! I'm the Paparazzi
2. Oops! I'm Up To Mischief
3. Oops! I'm the Paparazzi, Again

The Bitch-Proof Suit series:
1. The Bitch-Proof Suit
2. The Bitch-Proof Romance
3. The Bitch-Proof Bride
4. The Bitch-Proof Wedding

Heather Park: Regency Romance
Dublin Girl
Why Are All The Good Guys Total Monsters?
I'm Holding Out For A Vampire Boyfriend

Action/Thriller books:

Knight in Miami
Agency Agenda
Love Him Forever
Someone Worse

Electric Shadows
The Strife Of Riley
Shadows Of Murder
Cast a Dark Shadow

Children's books:

Faeriefied
Secondhand Spooks
Poison-Wynd

Wormhole Wynd
Science Fashion
School For Aliens

Colouring books:

Summer Nature
Flower Nature
Summer Garden
Spring Garden
Autumn Garden
Sea Dream
Festive Christmas
Christmas Garden
Christmas Theme

Flower Bee
Wild Garden
Faerie Garden Spring
Flower Hunter
Stargazer Space
Bee Garden
Scottish Garden
Seasons

Embroidery Design books:

Sea Theme Embroidery Patterns
Floral Garden Embroidery Patterns
Christmas & Winter Embroidery Patterns
Floral Spring Embroidery Patterns
Floral Nature Embroidery Designs
Scottish Garden Embroidery Designs

Printed in Great Britain
by Amazon